Walking Among the Unseen

WALKING AMONG THE UNSEEN

Hannah Hurnard

Tyndale House Publishers, Inc.
Wheaton, Illinois

This book comprises excerpts from
the following booklets by Hannah Hurnard
and is published by permission of the author:
Oh! What Fortunate People!
How to Develop Our Spiritual Senses
Green Pastures and Still Waters
The Secret of a Transformed Life
The Heavenly Powers
Somebody's Knocking
The Shining Hour of Departure

Library of Congress Catalog Card Number 77-072435
ISBN 0-8423-7805-7, paper
Copyright © 1977 by Tyndale House Publishers, Inc.,
Wheaton, Illinois. All rights reserved.
Printed in the United States of America

20 21 22 23 24 92

Contents

A Word of Introduction...

This is a book for people who are carrying heavy burdens. Burdens of sickness, fear, anxiety, weariness, mental strain, nervous exhaustion, sorrow, loneliness, pain, poverty, or whatever other kind of burden it may be. It brings the best possible Good News of a Helper, Deliverer, and Healer who shows us how to remake our individual worlds of experience through faith in and commitment to Jesus Christ.

For in God, the Creator of good things, we truly "live, and move, and have our being." In him there is nothing but goodness and health and abundant supply of all our possible needs. We must learn to transfer this glorious truth into living fact, and to make contact with that inexhaustible supply of power and love by joining the great company of people of whom Jesus spoke when he said, "What fortunate [or blessed] people you are if you know how to enter and live in the Kingdom of God."

Even if at present you are one of those unfortunate people who cannot believe in the existence of God, never mind. So was I. This book is for you too. For it tells you how to put Christianity to the test and to find, beyond shadow of doubt, that God is—and that he loves you and can relieve you of every kind of burden which you bear.

CHAPTER 1
God's Kingdom Is Here

"Be ye transformed by the renewing of your mind" (Romans 12:2).

What an exciting and wonderful thing it is to become a transformed creature—like a caterpillar emerging from the chrysalis and finding itself transformed into a glorious winged creature, able to live in another world altogether—a sky world instead of an earthly one!

Just such a wonderful transformation

happened in my own life some years ago, and I would like to tell you about it. It took place when I understood the meaning and significance of this verse and began to experience it. I became a transformed person through a completely transformed thought-life. I began to think about and react to everything that happened to me in a completely new way.

In the Bible there is a beautiful story of a man who received a miraculous healing, and one of the comments made on that healing was: "The man was above forty years old on whom this miracle was performed." Well, so was I, for when this miraculous transformation in my life began, I was forty-six years old.

Like many other middle-aged people, I was growing very dissatisfied with myself and my life. I meant so well and longed to be of use, but somehow I seemed to be so dreadfully powerless, so unable to help people in their sorrows, sufferings, and sicknesses as I longed to do, and as I believe we are all meant to be able to do.

I talked about this lack of power to the Lord, and it seemed to me that he said to me in my thoughts, with gentle love and understanding, "Child, you need a complete transformation in your way of thinking about things, and in your habits of speech. You need to begin thinking and speaking as we do in heaven, instead of the way you have become accustomed to do on earth. Now I want you to become a real citizen of the Kingdom of heaven, and to rise to life in a new world altogether.

"First of all, child, you must understand that in the Kingdom of heaven no one majors on the faults and failures of other people, or the irritating or wrong things that they do. We speak of 'things that are true ... honest ... just ... pure ... lovely ... of good report,' about special virtues and things which deserve praise (Philippians 4:8). These are the things to think about. So begin with this rule. Don't feed yourself a constant diet of thoughts about the things that you don't like or don't agree with, or of which you disapprove, or which cause you to feel irritation, anger, resentfulness, jealousy, or any other unlovely feelings."

"O Lord!" I said, almost in despair. "I am forty-six years old, and my thought-habits are fixed. All my life I have been eagle-eyed in the matter of seeing the faults and blemishes in other people; and when I see them, I not only can't stop thinking about them, but I point them out to other people and deplore them. Often I even suggest that some of us should pray together about the annoying persons, and ask that their faults should be clearly brought to their attention, so that they shall cease to be a stumbling-block to other people. Is this wrong?"

"My child, what is your motive? To help or hurt? Instead of blaming people, bless them, speak well of them. Concentrate on discovering the good things in people and on encouraging them to enjoy doing good and lovely things. You can't force people to stop doing bad things, but you can make doing good so attractive that they don't want to waste a minute of time on the wrong and harmful things. Try this method yourself, child, and see what a transformation it will bring about in your own life and in your power to help other people. You have already discovered that complaining about the things you don't like only fixes them still more deeply in your consciousness, so that the offending persons (even after you have prayed about their faults) only irritate you all the more each time you meet them, and so the situation gets worse and worse. Now concentrate on thinking of good and beautiful things and talk about them, expressing appreciation of everything good which you see (people respond to encouragement as flowers do to the sun). Quietly adapt yourself to living happily with the people who aggravate you, rather than trying to force them to change their habits so as to suit you."

"But, Lord, that sounds dreadful! When I am upset about something, I just have to get things off my chest. If I am not allowed to do that and must repress my feelings, I am afraid I shall explode or make myself ill."

"Not at all," said my loving Lord. "You must not repress anything, but simply change it into another feeling altogether.

14

When you are tempted to grumble, complain, or feel sorry for yourself, change that feeling into one of praise and thanksgiving."

"Lord, how can I praise and thank you despite really wrong or mean and spiteful things, or disappointments, or catastrophes?"

"It is very simple, child. You must just think thankfully that the bad and wrong thing gives you a wonderful opportunity to react to it in the heavenly way—as Jesus would—and so be able to bring something good out of a situation which looks so dreadfully wrong. Whenever you react with praise and thanksgiving for an opportunity to grow more like Jesus in your way of reacting to things, instead of grumbling or feeling self-pity, you will find that the whole situation will be changed into a great big blessing; whereas grumbling and complaining always make matters worse. So go through each day praising and thanking God no matter what happens, for this puts you in contact with his power.

"Then there is another thing for you to understand. In the Kingdom of heaven nobody ever gossips or talks about other people's private affairs and concerns. No one passes remarks about neighbors behind their backs. No comments of ill will are made about anything, not even politicians, or the minister at church, or the dreadful singing, or the way in which the committee

15

members disagreed, or the quarreling that goes on between Mrs. So-and-so and her husband or neighbor."

"Lord, does that mean that if I hear some spicy little tidbit I mustn't pass it on? I simply love to be the first person to bring a piece of such news to others!"

"Ah, child, it depends on what the little tidbit or piece of news is. You can't live in the Kingdom of heaven until the taste to share unlovely tidbits is changed. But if you hear that something has been done which is specially kind or noble or generous, you may certainly be the first person to report it. But never say or report anything which you would not like others to think or say about you behind your back. Heavenly people want to encourage and inspire others, not to bedaub them.

"Another thing—in heaven we don't picture ourselves doing wonderful things while other people look on admiringly. And no one shows off by letting others know how his efforts to serve are being used. Child, you, very specially, need to beware of this, because under the guise of persuading yourself that you only talk about your lovely opportunities and answered prayers, you are really being tempted to advertise that you are being used in a special way and that you are one of heaven's pets and favorites."

"Lord, that's simply frightful!"

"Yes, it really is, and you must beware of it."

"But are not people encouraged and strengthened in faith when they hear about answers to prayer and the way in which 'all our needs are supplied'?"

"Yes, if it is told at the right time and in the right place, but not when it is a public 'showing off.' That generally irritates people, or else just sounds like an interesting story which they enjoy hearing, but which has no practical effect on their lives. To share with individuals something which will meet their need at a particular time, and to encourage them in faith, is truly helpful. But you will notice that in the Gospels none of the Evangelists tell about anything that they did themselves when they went out preaching and healing in the villages. They tell nothing of how I used them personally. They remembered the warning of their Lord in Matthew 6:1-18, that they should do everything 'in secret' and not 'to be seen of men' or to be known about by other people."

"Then, Lord, now that you have explained all this to me, how can I, at the age of forty-six, be enabled to change my thought- and speech-habits in this drastic way?"

"Simply by faith; and that means that you must believe that this Kingdom of heaven way of life, which Jesus summed up so perfectly in the Sermon on the Mount and in his own life, is the ideal standard for everyone. You must definitely accept it as your own. This is faith—to believe what has been revealed through Jesus Christ, and to agree that this must be the standard for your own life. This faith will put you in contact with my power, and then you can 'be transformed by the renewing of your mind.' Don't depend on your own efforts to change your thought-habits, but on my power working in you.

"Just one more thing—never refuse to forgive. Forgiveness is the mightiest power of all, and you must joyfully practice it continually. It means willingness to bear everything that other people do to you, and to loose them in your thoughts from the wrong that they have done to you or spoken about you. When you loose the wrongdoer in your own thoughts, you will find, first, that you have loosed yourself from unhappy and harmful emotions, so that instead of being hurt, you will be blessed. But if you do not forgive men their debts, you will be bound to resentful, angry, grudging feelings which harm you. Remember—your reactions to your enemy can hurt you more than your enemy can."

God's message to me led the way to a renewed mind, a renewed commitment, a transformed life. Such growth experiences are a welcome relief from the drudgery we too often content ourselves with in our daily living.

Once there was a little boy (so the story goes) who lived in a house on the top of a hill. One morning when he ran outside to go down the hill to school, he stopped dead in his tracks and stared—for there, on the top of a hill on the other side of the valley, he saw a house with windows made of gleaming gold, flashing in the sunshine like an enchanted palace in a fairy tale. Where had it come from? How did it get there? Who lived in it? What fortunate people they must be to have glorious golden windows instead of ordinary glass ones! What wonderful treasures there must be inside such a mansion.

All that day he couldn't fix his attention on anything else. When at last school was over, he decided that instead of going straight home, he would climb the other hill and visit the house with the golden windows.

So off he went, and climbed and climbed until at last he reached the top of the hill. He looked around eagerly for the house he had seen. But there was nothing there but an ordinary house, and a kind-faced woman standing at the garden gate with a little girl about his own age beside her.

Panting and perspiring but full of eagerness, he asked the woman where the house with the golden windows was to be found. She looked very surprised and said, "There is no such house on this hilltop. Indeed, ours is the only one and, as you can see, it has ordinary glass windows." Then seeing how dreadfully crestfallen and disappointed he looked, she said kindly, "Never mind! Come inside and I will give you and my little girl a glass of lemonade each, and a piece of cake, and you can eat it together in the garden."

So the children sat together in the garden until it was evening and time for him to go home, and he poured out to the little girl all about the entrancing house which he had seen. Certainly it must have been a fairy one, for apparently it could appear and disappear. Oh, what fortunate people must own it, and how disappointed he was not to have found it, but he was determined to look for it every day until he could find it at last.

The little girl listened with wide-open, understanding eyes, nodding her head from time to time, and when he had finished she said mysteriously, "Well, there really is a house with golden windows, though Mommy doesn't know about it. But I have seen it, too, and it's just splendid. Only it isn't on this hilltop but on another one. Come with me and I will show you."

They went together to the garden gate and the little girl pointed and truly, there, away on another hilltop, there was a house with glorious flashing golden windows, so dazzling that the boy kept blinking his eyes as he looked at them.

"Isn't it beautiful!" said the little girl wistfully. "Oh, how I wish that I could live in a house with golden windows, for I am sure that they must look out onto a beautiful fairy world instead of this ordinary one!"

Then the little boy, still staring incredulously, exclaimed, "But that's my house. There are the two big pine trees, one on each side of the house, and I can see my mother taking the laundry off the clothesline."

Then, as they both stared in amazement, the sun sank a little lower and one by one the shining golden windows disappeared as they no longer reflected its rays, and the house became just the ordinary, safe, happy little home which he knew so well. His mother must be wondering anxiously where he had gone, and he must go home at once. So he said "Good-bye" to the little girl, promising to return to play with her again, and ran down the hill and up the other, and told his mother the whole curious story. When he had finished, she smiled at him lovingly and said, "Well, you know, I really do believe that we are very fortunate, and that we do live in a house with golden windows, because the love of God comes shining into them each day, and it is that which makes us so happy together and makes ordinary things bring us so much joy. If you understand this you will find, as Daddy and I have done, that we do live in a world more beautiful and wonderful than any fairyland, because we let God help us to make good and happy things happen instead of sad and bad ones, and you will learn to help us make them too."

I read the story about the house with the golden windows when I was a little girl, and that is a long time ago. But as the years have passed, and in a special way quite recently, I too have become one of "the fortunate people," and I too live in a house with golden windows—and doors—opening out, not into an unreal fairy story world, but into the glorious world of the Kingdom of God, filled with good and beautiful things and where blessed and happy things happen, because I have been fortunate enough to learn the secret of letting God make everything in it. As he is the creator of very good things, it becomes happier and more fortunate all the time!

To some, my life is ordinary and typical. But because God is in it, it is actually exciting and always new. It has golden windows.

Because my own world of personal experience is so full of happy things, again and again during the course of each day I find myself exclaiming, "Oh, what a fortunate person I am!" I long to share with other people who feel that they are not at all fortunate, but live in difficult and unhappy worlds, the lovely secret of how they too can join the company of fortunate people dwelling in the Kingdom of God.

What does it mean to live in the Kingdom of God? Today it is argued by good, religious people that the Sermon on the Mount is not meant to be obeyed in this Christian era at all. It will only be incumbent upon us when God's Kingdom has been actually established upon earth, and it is quite impossible to live according to it now in this fallen world. But in that case, why ever did Jesus come with such a challenge 2,000 years (at least) before anyone would be willing or able to respond to it and live according to the Kingdom of heaven standard!

For that is the amazing and glorious message he brought: "Repent and enter the Kingdom of heaven now. I have come to teach you how to live as God really wants you to live, as real citizens of his Kingdom, even while you are still here in human bodies on earth, and not in the way that fallen mankind has become accustomed to. Let God's will rule in every part of your life instead of self-will. If you will repent of all the things which you have done to others which you would not like them to do to you, and live devoting yourself to goodness only, and react to everyone and everything that happens to you in the heavenly ways that I am teaching you, you will discover that you are creating for yourselves new worlds of individual and corporate experience in which good and blessed things will be manifest. Then the joys of the heavenly life will begin for you even while you are here on earth, and the healing of your sorrows and sicknesses will take place, just as I am able to demonstrate to you as soon as you believe me, and respond to the challenge I am giving you, and are willing to live according to this higher Kingdom of heaven way of life."

Oh, what a glorious message it was he brought. And how wonderfully he was able to demonstrate and prove that it was true. For those who believed his message *were* healed of their sicknesses, *were* delivered from all the harmful things which spoiled their lives and kept them in bondage to wrong things, and they *did* receive power to begin living a life more abundant and more gloriously satisfying than anything which human beings had experienced before.

No one else had ever gone about "doing good and healing all that were oppressed of the devil," and curing the physical sicknesses and crippling infirmities of those who sought such aid. But Jesus was literally able to do this.

I remember hearing of a meeting of godly men who were earnestly debating this point, and one brother sought to prove conclusively that the teaching of the Sermon on the Mount was never meant for this gospel age at all and was, indeed, quite impossible to practice now as a way of life, for it would inevitably mean that the wicked took advantage of it and the righteous would be at a complete disadvantage. Quite other principles involving force, resistance, and law courts were obviously the right way of dealing with those who wrong us during this age when, unhappily, the Kingdom of heaven is not established on earth.

When he sat down, another member of the meeting stood and said gently, "Brother, I only want to ask you one thing. In the Millennium, when everyone is practicing the laws of the Kingdom of heaven, who is going to smite you on the right cheek and give you the opportunity to turn the left to him? Who is going to sue you and wrongfully take away your coat and give the opportunity to yield up your cloak also and so teach and demonstrate to him the heavenly principles? And when will you have opportunity in the Millennium to be made like your Master and Lord by loving your enemies and praying for them which despitefully use you and persecute you?"

To postpone the keeping of the laws of heaven until the Kingdom of heaven has really come on earth in all its perfection is to miss the whole point of the teaching and preaching of the Savior. For it is through men and women actually practicing these heavenly principles in a world which normally practices others diametrically opposed to the heavenly ones, that the kingdoms of this world are to be challenged and, through open demonstration, are to become convinced that the heavenly ones are the only laws which really work. This is the means by which men are to be attracted and challenged to enter the Kingdom of heaven themselves.

What is the Kingdom of heaven?

It is not by coincidence, but of set purpose that in both the Hebrew and Greek Scriptures the word "heaven" is used not only of God's dwelling place, but also of the firmament or sky which we see above our heads, and also of the starry heavens far beyond. For the heavens which are so much higher than the earth have always been chosen as the most fitting picture or symbol of the highest and most blessed state possible to men, a life in union with the life of God and in harmony with his laws. Whenever we speak of heaven, we instinctively look upward toward a higher sphere and a higher plane of life than this earthbound plane on which we live. The name heaven sums up man's highest aspirations and longings after God. Therefore, heaven is that blessed and highest state of all where God reigns supreme, with no rebels resisting his will, but only joyful cooperation on the part of all.

Therefore the Kingdom of heaven is everywhere where God's will is loved and obeyed.

When we get into the Kingdom of heaven, we find that it is, in fact, the Kingdom of love, for in it there is only one Law, "the royal law" of love (James 2:8). Heaven is where God dwells and "God is love" (1 John 4:16). God dwells in us, and the Kingdom of heaven has been extended into our lives. We have been annexed as it were and made a part of heaven ourselves. The only way that the Kingdom of heaven can come on earth is by coming in the lives of men and women everywhere.

When the Lord preached that "the Kingdom of heaven is at hand," he meant that the time had come for God's Kingdom to begin to be established on earth through the men and women who would enter into it, become part of it, and thus establish it wherever they were by obeying its one law of love and practicing the principles of love, in opposition to the principles of this fallen and rebellious world. We become citizens of heaven by accepting God's reign in our own lives. By so doing, we find ourselves raised up to the highest level of life possible to men, and living in harmony with God's universal law of love.

Our Lord taught the way up to the gate of the Kingdom of heaven!

"Jesus began to preach, and to say, Repent: for the Kingdom of heaven is at hand" (Matthew 4:17).

Repentance begins in the thoughts and imaginations of the heart, which are evil continually. Our habitual thought-life, the inner secret life that we, each one, live, is the very heart of our trouble. We think selfishly and according to worldly ideas, and we must now begin to think in the heavenly way. And this involves thinking about the ways in which we have broken the heavenly law of love, and are therefore, in actual fact, living outside God's Kingdom as rebels against him.

How many Christians there are who need a revolution in their thought-life and in their understanding of the real meaning of the Kingdom of heaven. For it is all too possible to call oneself a "believer" in Jesus Christ and yet to know little or nothing about living as a citizen in the Kingdom of heaven. It is possible to be most earnest and prayerful that we may be saved and kept from living an inconsistent Christian life, and yet at the same time to know nothing about practicing the heavenly principles of the Kingdom in daily life, but to live by completely different standards than the heavenly ones, and therefore in actual fact and of necessity to be living a life far below that of the Kingdom of heaven.

The Lord Jesus described the true citizens of the Kingdom of heaven by a most lovely name, and they are the only people who have the right to such a name. He called them "the blessed ones" or as a quite literal translation would express it, "the happy people"; for blessed does mean happy in the sense of being perfectly whole and perfectly in harmony with God's will and purposes for us. No wonder the gospel is "glad tidings," for it tells us how we may become the "happy people," citizens of the Kingdom of heaven.

CHAPTER 2
King of Love

Imagine how those multitudes of unfortunate people who flocked to Jesus felt when he showed them the way into the Kingdom. Until then, they had lived in a dreadfully dark and unhappy world. Many of them were cripples or suffered from painful diseases. They had no medical services such as we have today, and no one to help them when they were mentally sick and suffering from fears and delusions which chained them to outbreaks of violence, causing other people to say that they were possessed by devils and unclean spirits. In those days, madness was generally treated with almost unbelievable cruelty.

Multitudes of other people were slaves, the absolute possession of their masters. Others were unfit for work and had to beg for their daily food, and multitudes were so weary and exhausted that they did not know how to drag themselves through each day as it came, feeling utterly unable to cope with the burdens and demands of life and in dread of breaking down altogether. Just like so many, many of us today! But Jesus was able to help them, and can, and will, help us too. He is the fullness of God's divine compassion and love, and again and again when he was talking to sad, sick, and desperate people about the Kingdom of God and how to enter it, he used these words—"Oh, what fortunate people you are, when you hear and do the things which I have come to teach you. I have brought you the best Good News possible. Come unto me all you who are weary and heavy laden, and I will give you rest. I will teach you how to enter the Kingdom of God."

It was such Good News and worked so wonderfully when people believed it and did what he taught them that they flocked in by the thousands to hear him and found that, in very fact, the Good News was true.

Tom, the chimney sweep in Charles

Kingsley's *Water-Babies,* after clambering up innumerable chimneys in a huge mansion, lost his way and instead of coming down the kitchen chimney, crawled out onto the hearth in a spotlessly white bedroom where a lovely little girl lay asleep between immaculately white sheets, in a room where not a speck of dirt was to be seen. Tom, the little orphan chimney sweep, gazed around him, enchanted by his first sight of such beauty and cleanness, having never imagined that anything so spotless and lovely could exist. Suddenly he caught sight of a filthy apelike little creature, sooty black from head to foot, standing on the rosy pink carpet with pools of black perspiration dripping from its body. It was such a shockingly incongruous object in such surroundings that he shook his fist at it and shouted furiously, "Get out of here at once!" But the black ape shook its fist in return and suddenly, for the first time in his life, poor little Tom realized that he was looking in a mirror and seeing himself as he really was. It broke his heart. Uttering a desolate and despairing cry, he rushed out of the house, sobbing as he went, "I must be clean! I must be clean! Where can I find a stream of water and wash and be clean!"

Isn't that exactly the effect which Jesus had upon his listeners as they looked upon him and for the first time saw the perfect ideal for all men and loathed themselves by contrast, and fell at his feet with the bitter cry, "Oh, if you will, make us clean!"

Jesus Christ proclaimed a triumphant message of forgiveness, when hungry, guilty masses came to hear him, and he gladly ministered to them.

By contrast, the Lord continually took his disciples away from the crowds which were attracted by his healing powers and never—no never—allowed them to advertise either his or their own preaching and healing! He seemed to have an aversion to advertising and publicity stunts. He would have nothing to do with the devil's suggestion that he should cast himself down from the pinnacle of the Temple in order to attract great crowds to listen to his message. Constantly he withdrew with his disciples into quiet places, and though the crowds often followed, they were quite unsought as far as devices for attracting them were concerned.

How did Jesus set about his stupendous task carrying out his mission of rescuing mankind from self-centered blindness? What method did he use when he rejected the world's method of destructive force and set out to reveal and demonstrate God's way of dealing with the problem of evil?

The answer is simple. He "went about doing good, and healing all that were oppressed of the devil; for God was with him" (Acts 10:38). He clearly stated his mission in these words: "God sent not his Son into the world to condemn the world; but that the world through him might be saved" (John 3:17). "I came not to judge the world, but to save the world" (John 12:17). So he went about everywhere preaching the gospel of the Kingdom of God, and calling upon men to enter it and to devote themselves to goodness—and thousands flocked to listen to his wonderful open-air preaching.

This too is a most extraordinary thing, though most of us have perhaps never stopped to think about it. How was it possible that in an enemy-occupied country, where open-air meetings of any kind were forbidden in case the population should be incited to rise against their conquerors, Jesus was permitted to speak to thousands of people in the open air? They hung upon his words, followed him from place to place, and openly hailed him as the son of David and therefore the true heir to the throne of Israel. How could he possibly get away with it without being arrested, imprisoned, and put to death, as had been the fate of so many would-be messiahs before him? For underground resistance movements and leaders there had been in plenty ever since the Romans conquered Palestine. But it is quite clear from the Gospels that the Roman authorities in Palestine permitted Jesus to travel about collecting vast crowds of listeners and holding open-air meetings in desert places as well as in towns and cities. What could happen today if people in enemy-occupied countries gathered crowds in deserted places and hailed somebody as true leader and deliverer of their nation! Then why did the Roman authorities, far from preventing all this, allow the teaching of Jesus to spread like wildfire all over the country?

Jesus never attacked, denounced, or spoke against the Roman authorities, never stirred up anyone to protest or resist the ruling invaders of his country. Rather, wherever he went, he taught God's way of reacting to, and dealing with, the cruel and unjust. Everywhere he went he gave the same challenge (as the authorities very well knew): "love your enemies," and your conquerors. Bear and forgive whatever they do to you. Turn them into friends by doing good to them unceasingly, until they just can't resist it and begin doing good to you too. "If your enemy hunger, give him food. If he thirst, give him drink. Show kindness whenever you receive unkindness and malice."

Just think how the Roman legionaries on duty at the open air meetings must have felt as they listened to that kind of challenge, and heard him say, "Even if you are forcibly taken from your work and compelled to carry a burden for the soldiers for a mile without payment (the Roman law permitted this to be done, and it was greatly resented by the conquered inhabitants of the country), do it cheerfully, and at the end of the mile offer to carry it further" (see Matthew

5:41). If you are struck in the face, don't hit back but accept it gently and forgivingly (v. 39). React to every wrong done to you in a good way, making it an opportunity for you to express the opposite goodness, and so to help goodness to show itself instead of evil. "Render therefore unto Caesar the things which are Caesar's; and unto God the things that are God's" (Matthew 22:21).

How would Roman centurions react to that? "Stop this man from teaching and preaching in public"? Most certainly not! "All of you who are hanging back in case you will be arrested, don't be afraid. Come and listen to this speaker and bring your neighbors. The more people who listen and respond to his teaching, the better for everybody concerned! We Romans won't have to do any more of the beastly work of flogging and crucifying resisters, and we shall have time and opportunity to learn to be gentle and kind and to do good ourselves." Among themselves they would say, "What does it matter if the people call him 'King of the Jews' instead of that puppet King Herod if he has no designs against Caesar and the Roman authorities? Let this king of love and goodness reign indeed. Caesar won't object, as long as they go on paying their taxes as this man tells them to do, and if they don't resist law and order. Let him rule in their hearts and, God grant it, in ours too!"

That is why Jesus was never arrested by

the Romans! Some of the national leaders of the conquered nation, who hated their conquerors, wanted to try to force or persuade Jesus to use his miraculous powers and hold over the people's hearts to incite an uprising against the Romans and to liberate the country from their power. When Jesus refused to do this—because they hated this kind of teaching instead of the agelong call to the use of arms and destructive force—they actually began plotting and trying to kill him themselves, first urging the Romans to forbid his teaching and to arrest him. When the Romans refused on several occasions, these politically minded leaders, religious and otherwise, tried to do away with Jesus themselves. Once they closed the gates of the Temple courtyard and collected a great pile of stones with which to stone Jesus to death. But they just couldn't throw the stones and he walked quietly away among the crowds of people who were gathered there. On another occasion, they tried to throw him over a precipice outside Nazareth, but they couldn't keep their hold on him, "and he, passing through their midst, went his way." Even the armed gang sent to the Garden of Gethsemane to arrest him secretly by night, when there would be no people about to protest and protect him, fell to the ground utterly helpless as soon as he stepped forward and said, "Here I am. I am the man you want." And when Peter struck out with a sword and cut off the ear of the high priest's servant (as a result of which all the disciples would have been immediately arrested and crucified as being armed terrorists masquerading as preachers and healers), Jesus intervened. He simply asked that one of his hands might be untied for a moment, bent down, picked up the severed ear, put it back on the man's head—and it healed immediately. Then Jesus said, "Let these go free," and again his captors did just what he told them, and none of the disciples were arrested. Jesus' goodness and kindness opposed and outshone his enemies' evil and cruel purposes.

Even then it still looked as though Jesus would be freed, for when his captors dragged their prisoner before Pilate, the Roman governor, he was horrified at the idea of putting Jesus to death and thus removing his wonderful influence for good and for peace. In the end it was only because the men who so hated Jesus threatened to send a message to Caesar in Rome, saying that his representative in Palestine was aiding and abetting a man who claimed to be king instead of Caesar, that Pilate, in deadly fear, agreed that Jesus should be crucified. He washed his hands in front of them all, saying, "Bear witness—I am free of the blood of this innocent man; it is you who condemn him to death."

Why did Jesus allow himself to be crucified? No one could have done it if he had not allowed it. His enemies had tried before, and had failed. He said plainly, "No man taketh it [my life] from me, but I lay it down of myself. I have power to lay it down, and I have power to take it again" (John 10:18). Why did he believe so clearly that he must give his life?

So that he could reveal, and triumphantly demonstrate, the truth that God bears and forgives the very worst that men can do, and that this is the only successful method of dealing with evil. Bear it and share in all its consequences with those who commit the wrong. Forgive them, love them, as Christ forgave and loved. Divine forgiveness, the greatest power in the universe, can be a force in us.

The incredible message of the Cross is this: God himself suffers with sinners in the consequences of their sins until he is able to destroy their self-centeredness forever. It is also his call and challenge to every one of us to realize that we must all be willing to bear and forgive the very worst which others may do to us and to our loved ones, for this is the only way to abolish evil. When we practice forgiving love, we shall be raised up to the highest place of power with Jesus, where we can unite with God our Father in drawing men to himself. We shall be empowered to cooperate in the lovely rescue work of heaven, just as the first disciples and followers of Jesus were sent out to preach this supremely Good News of overcoming evil.

What method did Jesus tell his followers to use to proclaim this gospel or Good News?

It was a profoundly simple method which anyone can use. It did not require any money, and no paid workers. It did not depend upon financial support and gifts from others. It needed no organizations, no paid publicity, no influential persons to support it. Such methods were not the ones he taught and used himself, simply because they are not so successful as the Kingdom ones and can too easily snare us into trusting in these things rather than in our Savior.

The one sure method of getting the message proclaimed to every creature on earth is simply this: each one of us is to practice the Kingdom of God way of life and to teach it and demonstrate it to each person we meet and with whom we are associated, and to seek to persuade them to practice it too. It is the "one by one, person to person" method, and it is absolutely foolproof! That is what the early disciples and Christians did. Wherever they went and wherever they lived and worked, they lived this Kingdom of God way of life, devoting themselves to goodness, and practicing forgiving love to all. They demonstrated in their own lives and healed bodies and health their power to heal and help others. They showed how gloriously it works, persuading others to enter the Kingdom of God too. The message spread like wildfire all over the known world in that first generation after Jesus Christ.

There is no better or more successful method to use today. Begin with the ordinary people you live and work with. Seek to bring them into the Kingdom of God, and the power and witness will spread further and further as individuals respond one after the other and find that God working in them is rebuilding their lives. What fortunate people we are to be among those who know this glorious secret and can demonstrate its blessedness. Come and join us and enter the kingdom of fortunate people too!

Another amazing fact is this—the King will someday, perhaps this very day, return for all those who know him personally, so they can actually be with him forever.

"They shall see the Son of Man coming in a cloud with power and great glory.... Then look up, and lift up your heads; for your redemption draweth nigh" (Luke 21:27, 28).

Some time ago I said to a friend, "I never see you walking on the beach now." And she replied, "Well, we generally drive to the end of the island and walk there. It is so delightful."

"Is it?" I answered. "I have always heard

that it is very noisy and crowded there and so I have avoided it."

She smiled and said, "You ought to go and see for yourself." And then she told me how to get there without going by the main road. Following her directions, I came into what seemed almost like a new country altogether. The tide was high, sailing boats were skimming over a portion of the estuary I had not seen before, and just across on the far bank was a little town whose presence was just where I had never suspected! Barges were steaming out to the North Sea, and only a few children played alone among the oak trees on the little cliffs. Yes, it really was as though I had found an enchanted door and walked into a new world.

Then I turned and looked inland, and suddenly I recognized where I was. I had been there before, or at least at the place where I was looking. More than fifty years ago, during the First World War, while we were still small children and my mother was alive, we had come here one Saturday for a picnic—and since that day, as far as I was concerned, the place had vanished from the earth! Yet really, of course, it had been there all the time, though I was unaware of it. Now it "appeared" before me again, accompanied by a vivid memory, as though it had been away in a far country and had now returned.

When this realization broke upon me, I

found my thoughts winging their way back through the years of memory to yet another country and another experience. I was in the Central Americas and had gone outside to look about me on my first day there. Great clouds blotted out any view which might have been visible on a clear day, and I could see nothing of the surroundings. But on the second morning as I started for a walk, I looked up and there, "coming in the clouds of heaven," "appearing" as they parted asunder, was a glorious circle of snow mountains, shining in the sunshine. I had never suspected their presence or existence. Yet they had been there all the time, actually exerting an influence over the whole area, helping to form the weather and to supply water for the city from their melting snows. Now here they were, "coming in the clouds," breaking in upon my delighted vision (for I have always been a passionate lover of snow-peaks), appearing as though from another world. But of course they had not come suddenly flying from afar—they had been there all the time, though I had not been able to see them. As I stood there, watching them "coming in all their glory," it broke upon me what a lovely illustration or parable this was to help me understand about the "coming again of the Lord" in power and glory; the "appearing" for which we wait with such joyful expectation and longing.

For, of course, he has never really been

away, any more than the mountains had been away from that city—he has only been hidden from our sight by the veil of our physical senses and our occasional unbelief. Did he not say to the friends who sorrowed because he told them that for a time they would see him no more, "Lo, I am with you alway, even unto the end of the world." In effect, he was saying, "You will not see me, but I shall be here still, and you must live and think and speak and act just as you would if you saw me visibly before you as you do now. Then, one day, you will be able to see me again, appearing as it were through rending clouds, as you are 'caught up' to a higher realm of spiritual awareness; either as you put off your mortal bodies in death and put on the new heavenly ones awaiting you, or by receiving power to be 'changed, in a moment, in the twinkling of an eye,' your bodies transfigured into heavenly ones without passing through disease and physical death."

Our human physical senses are able to perceive only such a tiny fraction of the spiritual realities all about us. We cannot see "an innumerable company of angels," or "the general assembly and church of the firstborn," or "the spirits of just men made perfect," or "Jesus the mediator of the new covenant" (Hebrews 12:22-24). But they are all there! And one glorious day, very soon now, the veil will be torn aside from our eyes and we shall see with wonder and joy what has been there all the time. All the heavenly hosts and Jesus our Lord himself will appear in power and glory; not as he was when he humbled himself to appear in the form of a human man, the carpenter of Galilee, the gracious teacher and the compassionate healer, but as he was when he rose triumphant from the grave, having overcome death and all the hosts of darkness, and as he ascended in his heavenly body.

Pondering joyfully on all this, I knew that there was still something else for him to show me. I got in the car and drove along the little twisting country road as far as it would go, and so came to the exact place we had visited in my childhood. There I stood remembering why for more than fifty years I had never returned to that spot. For, you see, on that Saturday long, long ago, I and my sisters had wanted to go to our favorite seaside resort much further away than this little island near our home. But it was wartime and gas was rationed, and my tired, busy mother had brought us to this place instead. It was not what I wanted, and the tide was out, and I remember how I grumbled and complained that there was nothing but mud, and nothing to do, and it was a horrible place, and I would never come here again. So I had spoiled the whole holiday for myself, and worse still, for our mother, who all too seldom went with us on picnics. It was the grumbling and complaining and resentment associated in my memory with that place, which, for a whole lifetime since, had made me decide I did not like the place, and so I had never returned to see it in all its enchanting beauty until that afternoon. What a parable that is also, as my gentle Lord pointed out. More than half a century is a long time to allow a spirit of grumbling and resentment to keep one away from happiness and from appreciation of God-created beauty. But that is just what such a spirit can do.

As we wait for his Coming, let us be careful that we do not give way to the habit of grumbling and resentment or criticism of others, or of complaint and anger, lest, when the glorious time comes, we sadly learn how much beauty and joy we missed in our living for him, or actually for ourselves.

How greatly we need to use the golden keys of penitence and of willingness to forgive others; and to be thankful and to wear the garment of praise instead of the spirit of heaviness or murmuring. For by means of such keys we can quicken our spiritual awareness, and can open the door to heavenly joys which we have long locked out of our lives by unheavenly attitudes and habits.

As I got into the car to drive back, I could hardly see because my eyes were full of tears. Not really tears of sorrow and regret, but of happy thankfulness. For I realized another glorious truth: when he appears and the heavenly world all about us breaks upon our quickened spiritual sight, we shall also see, once again, those we knew and have lost awhile. See them, not just as they were while in their human bodies, with their own human frailties and temptations, but as they really longed to be in the depths of their hearts. And when they appear again before us, will not one of our sweetest heavenly joys be just this—not that we can tell them how sorry we are for the times we hurt them (I think there will be no need for that), but that there will be so many beautiful opportunities and ways by which to express the appreciation and gratitude and love we either withheld, or seemed unable to express, while they were still on earth. Even better yet, we will see Christ and be able to fully express our love to him.

Yes, that bright and glorious day is very near now when his own promise will be fulfilled: "I will see you again, and your heart shall rejoice, and your joy no man taketh from you" (John 16:22).

I expect that sometimes, just like myself, you wake in the night or early morning and find yourself thinking of all the countless multitudes of human beings around the world who are kept from sleep through terror or pain or hunger, or because they cannot lie down in safety anywhere. Or, waking from troubled sleep, they must face another day of fear and anguish, with no human power to help them in their need or to rescue them. And you find your soul crying out in longing, "Come quickly, Lord Jesus!"

Surely that prayer, like all true prayers, is not simply an entreaty, but also a challenge and even a call from the Lord, to help him in fulfilling the prayer! For we must help to prepare the way of the Lord and to make ready a people prepared for him.

capable of receiving impressions of quite other kinds, a whole new and vast world or universe, of which we are now completely unconscious, would come breaking in upon our perceptions—a world of being, in fact, which is there all the time although we have no avenues or perceptions whereby to become aware of it—a spiritual world.

In every age and generation, multitudes of men and women have claimed that through experiencing "a new birth" they have recovered their lost spiritual organs of perception and they have come to know that other world as intimately and as realistically as they know this one of the lower senses. All these witnesses maintain most emphatically that our prison house of this world (the cosmos) is, in fact, right in the midst of the heavenly world, is indeed a part of it. But because we prisoners of this sensual world have lost all the vital avenues of perception by means of which that spiritual world can alone be known, we are like blind and deaf men as far as that vaster realm is concerned. Nevertheless, we too are "naked and open" to the eyes, not only of God himself, but of all holy, spiritual beings who are the inhabitants of that blessed world. The Bible is full of such witnesses, but one of the most striking perhaps is that of Elisha who, when his terrified servant saw only the soldiers and horsemen of their enemies in this world, prayed, "Lord, I pray thee, open his eyes, that he may *see*. And the

Lord opened the eyes of the young man; and he *saw;* and, behold, the mountain was full of horses and chariots of fire round about Elisha" (2 Kings 6:17).

Why must things to do with the eternal world always be so unreal to people who have not been born again, and why can't such people be given tangible proof of the other world? Because they have no spiritual senses through which to perceive it, so it must remain completely undemonstrable to them. Those who have developed their spiritual senses speak with unshakable assurance and authority about the reality of the other world. It is so real to them that multitudes of them have cheerfully and triumphantly suffered martyrdom with that world open all around them, with its inhabitants waiting to welcome them as they "fell asleep" to the consciousness of this world and walked out alive and exulting into the next one!

Perhaps the many Bible verses about "the world" confuse you, as they once did me.

"Love not the world, neither the things that are in the world. If any man love the world, the love of the Father is not in him. For all that is in the world, the lust of the flesh, and the lust of the eyes, and the pride of life, is not of the Father, but is of the world. And the world passeth away, and the desire thereof: but he that doeth the will of God abideth for ever" (1 John 2:15-17).

"The friendship of the world is enmity with God" (James 4:4).

Yes, the world of the cosmos, this poor prison house of the five senses, is a very passing affair—for as soon as the body dies, this world ceases to exist as far as the soul is concerned. What folly, therefore, to set one's love and supreme value on the things perceived only by the physical senses, and to remain completely unaware of, and unappreciative of, the eternal world which will never pass away and which lies all about us.

On the other hand, "God so loved the world" (the world of these poor men locked up in the prison house of their sense impressions alone) that he sent his Son into the prison house to bring back to us the life by means of which we may become aware of the world of heaven all around us, and be able at last to walk out into it free men and women at home in that blessed world with which, before, we could have no contact.

By the time I understood that the glorious experience of new birth restored to me the lost spiritual senses by which the real world can be known, I began praying most earnestly, longing to be taught how to develop, exercise, and use those senses in such a way that my own miserable materialism might be done away with completely and life in the heavenly places would become a real experience. It is these further lovely discoveries which I long now to share with others.

I do not mean that we ought to see visions or visual images, or hear audible voices, but that we are meant to enjoy and experience the glorious equivalents of these things in a spiritual way. It is true that the Apostle Paul was caught up into the heavens in spiritual ecstasy, and John the Apostle saw marvelous visions, and so did many of the prophets. So, likewise, have various other Christians in every succeeding age. But it is not of these abnormal and unusual experiences that I wish to write, for I personally have never experienced any such things. The things of which I now want to write are the experiences which ought to be normal to every Christian who "by reason of use" has developed his or her spiritual "senses" (Hebrews 5:14). Scripture uses our physical senses as illustrations of our spiritual senses.

It is interesting to notice how definitely the writer to the Hebrews refers to each of these spiritual senses:

The sense of spiritual hearing—"We have many things to say, and hard to be uttered, seeing ye are dull of *hearing*" (Hebrews 5:11).

The sense of spiritual sight—"...those who were once *enlightened* ... and were made partakers of the Holy Ghost" (Hebrews 6:4).

The sense of spiritual taste—"...have *tasted* of the heavenly gift ... and have *tasted* the good word of God, and the powers of the world to come" (Hebrews 6:4, 5).

53

The sense of spiritual smell—"...those who ... have their senses exercised to *discern* both good and evil" (Hebrews 5:14).

The sense of spiritual touch—"...*lay hold* upon the hope set before us" (Hebrews 6:18).

When I began to understand this and to check up on the development of my own spiritual senses, I was horrified to discover that even after years of being a Christian worker, some of these spiritual senses scarcely seemed to be functioning in me at all! No wonder, then, that the spiritual world seemed so unreal, so far away, and my whole life so strangely out of touch with heavenly realities except at certain special times. I began to see how tragically possible it is to find "retarded development" in the lives even of earnest Christian people. Are some of us perhaps still like newborn babes lying in a cradle or baby carriage while the sounds of the eternal world flow over us like a stream of words which convey no meaning or significance to us at all? To have only the faculties and powers of newborn infants, although to be in reality much older in age, is a real tragedy. Not for this were we born again of the Holy Spirit, insists the Apostle Paul most earnestly. He urges rather that we should "be no more children ... carried about ... [but should] grow up into him in all things ... till we come ... unto the measure of the stature of the fulness of Christ" (Ephesians 4:14, 15, 13).

These, then, are the spiritual senses which we are urged to develop and "exercise" (Hebrews 5:14), by means of which the unseen spiritual world, knowable only to the new creature or inner man, born again of the Spirit of God, can become the real homeland and true country of our souls. Then when the time comes to leave these bodies, we shall feel as much at home there as though we had been living there all the time—which is exactly the case!

There are five secret portals, whence
   The earthbound soul may flee
From this low prison house of sense,
And winging out and up from thence
   In the real world be free,
The realm of heaven—of love's control,
The native homeland of the soul.

Lord, give to us love-opened eyes;
   Give too a hearing heart,
By strong desire compelled to rise
And touch the things of Paradise;
   To enter where Thou art,
And taste the joys of heavenly powers,
And scent the perfume of its flowers.

Obedience is the hearing ear,
   Love is the seeing eye;
Responsive to thy voice we hear,
Responsive to thy love draw near
   And heavenly things descry.
Accepting thy dear plans, we feel
The joys of things unseen, but real.

A weaned heart which no longer clings
    To treasured earthly store
Receives from God the gift of wings
To rise and taste of heavenly things
    And love them more and more.
Through Love's transforming thoughts,
    we learn
'Twixt God and Evil to discern.

These are the senses of the soul,
    The gates that open wide;
By these the spirit is made whole,
And from this prison house control
    Is freed to pass outside.
Grant, Lord, these suffer no abuse,
But grow by exercise and use.

By the new birth we see and begin living in the real world, the spiritual realm. But, of course, we also continue to walk and talk in the physical world, where we rub shoulders with other people, most of whom remain blind to spiritual things.

As children of God, members of his Kingdom, we are responsible to treat others in a manner that is consistent with our spiritual calling, a calling that doesn't allow constant downgrading of those around us. Rather, we are responsible to love them.

Sometimes when I talk to people about this, or excuse myself from a conversation that I feel is unfair to another (usually absent) person, I am misunderstood. I believe that unfair attitudes toward or talk about others will bring evil consequences, whether bodily illness or destroyed friendships. "Oh, but that's like blackmail! God is trying to compel us to be good by threatening to punish us if we are not good," someone objects.

But as a matter of fact all this has nothing to do either with punishment of evil or reward for virtue. It is rather a matter of sowing and reaping (Galatians 6:7). For example, if we constantly criticize others, our friendships (or lack of genuine ones) will show it. It is quite true, as the Bible says, that "the fear of the Lord is the beginning of wisdom," and there is nothing wrong in a small child wanting to be good because he knows unpleasant consequences will follow if he is disobedient, as, for example, touching a hot poker when he has been warned not to do so. But once that child grows up, the motivations for his behavior should be more positive. And as we mature spiritually, we long to let God inspire all that we think and say and do. It becomes the greatest delight possible to us and we can only exclaim again and again, "O how I love thy law! It is my meditation all the day" (Psalm 119:97). Then we cooperate with the law, not through fear, but exulting in being fortunate enough to personally know the one who helps us obey it.

We too often mix evil with goodness when we are talking about other people and describing them to our friends and acquaintances. For example, how often we say such things as the following: "She is ever such a good-hearted woman, but simply hopeless as cook and housekeeper." Or, "He is an excellent person, but exasperatingly untidy and unpunctual." Or, "No doubt they mean well, but they have the stupidest ideas." Or, "Well, that group may be very zealous in good works toward their fellowmen, but they are quite unsound in their religious beliefs and teaching." That kind of thing. It's not necessarily wrong to see another's faults, but must we tell a third party about them? What are our motives?

Perhaps you're saying, "People need to be told these things or they cannot know the facts of the case." For example, "It will help you to realize what this person is up against and you will be able to pray for her more understandingly if I tell you that she devotes herself to looking after a bedridden old parent who is quite helpless and frightfully selfish, demanding, and cantankerous. If you don't know this, you cannot realize how difficult it is for her."

Is not the very fact that she devotes herself to a frail, bedridden person enough to give insight into the situation? Does adding the part about the parent being selfish and cantankerous really help one to be sympathetic? Perhaps a good test is, Am I merely mentioning someone's weaknesses, or am I also praying about them?

How quickly this way of mixing evil with good can become a habit of which we can all too easily remain completely unconscious! We are prone to do it all the time when talking to our friends and acquaintances, and still more when talking to ourselves in thought! But there are some important things to be noticed about it.

Mere criticism has absolutely no power to help the people we are talking about. It will do nothing to make it easier for them to escape from destructive habits or selfish demands or erroneous beliefs. Criticism unaccompanied by actions designed to help can be classed with the "idle words" (namely useless and uncreative ones) against which Jesus warns us in Matthew 12:36: "I say unto you, That every idle word that men shall speak, they shall give account thereof in the day of judgment."

Also, by spouting off about someone else, we are likely to harm the people we are talking too, infecting them with prejudice against people they either have not seen or in whom they themselves have not noticed such faults. It is a terrible thing to infect the minds of other people and thus poison others' personal relationships.

We certainly harm ourselves by unfairly putting others down too. Almost certainly we will be hurt by discovering that other people are passing unkind judgments on us behind our backs, and poisoning other people against us too. Our Lord most clearly warns us in these words: "Judge not, that ye be not judged. For with what judgment ye judge, ye shall be judged."

I remember visiting a sweet-faced old

lady approaching her ninetieth birthday. She lives in a home for retired people and, to tell the truth, I had heard that some of the other elderly people who lived there were not very happy about the way it was run. So while we were having lunch together, I began my questioning. How did she like living where she now was, instead of in her own home?

She said happily, "Oh, I can't speak too highly of this place. Everybody is so kind, and we are so well cared for."

I was a little disconcerted at hearing this different version of the case and said tentatively, "I have heard that there is a continual change of personnel. Different chiefs of staff and helpers coming and going all the time?"

"Well, that is so," she conceded cheerily. "It seems very difficult nowadays to find any permanent helpers. But while they are with us, they are all very nice and kind. For instance, the nurse who is with us at present is very young indeed. She looks a mere girl, and one would think she would find it very dull and dreary, looking after old people. But you know, she is just lovely to me. It seems that there is nothing too much trouble for her to do."

I looked at the sweet, contented old face before me and made a mental note. It seems that if you learn to be contented, grateful, and appreciative, you help to bring the best out in other people, and you are not likely to have a lonely and neglected old age. Especially if you also learn to ignore quietly, and without protest, the things you find not very much to your liking, and concentrate on making the best of everything.

How should we treat others, whether or not they share with us membership in the Kingdom of God?

We should willingly give a loving welcome to all who come seeking the shelter of an understanding heart. I remembered what another friend said—"If you have someone to love and to be loved by, you can never be really lonely and unhappy." More about her later. I prayed, "Dear Lord, please teach me to welcome everyone and to think lovingly about them. Help me to forgive those who hurt me, or seem to neglect me: forgiving them not just for the things they say and do, but also for being the sort of people they are."

Also, as Jesus stressed so emphatically, we must always forgive everything unjust or mean or unkind done to us by others, in the same way that we want God to forgive our own wrongdoing. It is deadly dangerous to allow a resentment or grudge or angry feeling to remain in us, especially overnight. "Let not the sun go down upon your wrath" (Ephesians 4:26). The real meaning of the word "forgive" is to loose and send away, and this is just what we are meant to do with all wrong attitudes and feelings: loose them out of the mind and memory and replace them with loving thoughts for the person who wounded our feelings or wronged us in some way. Ask God to forgive that person just as you want him to forgive you for all that you think and say and do which is self-inspired and harmful to others. Then refuse to think further about the matter or to speak about it to anyone—for what we speak about and tell others, we impress more deeply in our memory and consciousness. Thus, telling others about the things that have caused us resentment and anger or hurt feelings only binds those things again to us in memory, and gives them power to go on arousing the diseased feelings and reactions, so that we poison ourselves over and over again. This doesn't exclude sharing and bearing one another's burdens, but again, what is our motive?

We must also share the Good News of the Kingdom of God with others, as soon as we begin to prove in personal experience that it really is true and does work. For it is evil and selfish to be content to enjoy it alone. It must be shared with others so that they too may be persuaded and helped to awaken from the unreal dream-life of their self-created worlds and to be born again. Then they too can experience all the wonder and joy of entering God's Kingdom, which is the only world that really matters.

CHAPTER 4
Living in a Dying World

"Stop sitting on the fence—do something to help alter all the evil in the world around you—change the terrible conditions under which the majority of people live!"

This cry of young people today, concerned about the evil and unjust conditions in this suffering world, expresses their impatient reactions to the older generation. And, of course, they are absolutely right—thank God for their challenge. Certainly, we are not to ignore the fact that terrible injustices, poverty, homelessness, ignorance, crime, and suffering abound everywhere, and that multitudes of appallingly unfortunate people are suffering in the self-created dream world of fallen, self-centered mankind. Are we just to leave them in their sufferings, hoping they will learn through such nightmare conditions to hate the evil which causes these hells on earth, while we live blissfully and uncaringly, fortunate enough to know how to create wonderful and safe little heavens of our own, oases of spiritual security?

No, indeed, God forbid! There can be no peace of conscience for any of us as long as we deliberately leave any soul, let alone multitudes of them, to suffer in self-made hells. Because that kind of neglect is, in itself, a mighty wrong and evil. It helps to create the very hells which we ignore and to which we shall, in some way, have to gravitate and share if we continue such neglect. No, we must realize with unutterable joy that heaven is one great rescue mission. The highest joy is the joy of being able to rescue others from their hells as Jesus did.

However, it is tremendously important not only to ask, "Why aren't we helping to change the evil condition in the world?" but also the still more important question, "How are we to change them? What is the successful method?" Indeed, is it really possible to destroy evil conditions in a self-centered world where every nation is intent on guarding its own rights and prosperity and feels that that is more important than anything else? We choose for our leaders and politicians those men who will put our own nation first and then see if perhaps there is something left over that can be spared to help the less fortunate ones, always provided that those who are helped will gratefully support their benefactors against rival powers. This is disgusting to God.

How can a world governed and controlled by a spirit of selfishness be rescued from the evils and sufferings which are the inescapable results of selfishness? (Selfishness is, of course, the foundation of all sins.) This is the problem which none of the world's leaders and politicians have been able to solve. And what unfortunate people such leaders are—to be involved in the ghastly horror of war, and not to know how to bring it to an end or to extricate one's nation as year after year the cost in armaments, suffering, and destruction grows ever greater. Or to be the leader of a backward nation, perhaps ravaged by famine or earthquake or poverty or economic troubles, and not to know how to set things right and alleviate the suffering and distress. Can there be anything more unfortunate than not knowing how to escape such evil?

The only method which the world has depended upon for trying to control evil has been the use of superior strength and destructive force: imprisoning criminals by force, piling up more and more destructive armaments than those possessed by other nations threatening our own, so that if possible they may be deterred by fear from attacking us, or if they do attack they may be completely destroyed. If your enemies are planning to do something against you, discover it and do it to them first! If they use devilish inventions which cause appalling suffering to countless innocent people, then grudge no cost in inventing and acquiring and using even more devilish ones, even though countless more innocent people will have to suffer as a result of it. That is the only answer to the problem which the world has known and used.

But long, heartbreaking millennia of depending on destructive force as a deterrent to evil and a means of preventing it have shown not only that it is a complete failure, but, far worse, that it has actually increased evil. But such measures alone, with wrong motivation, merely increase the problem.

What is the best method of dealing with the evils of want and poverty and homelessness, and for helping the victims of terrible natural disasters? Although relief work and generous sharing of what we have with those in distress is very good as far as it goes, most relief workers would be the first to admit that, though it is possible to alleviate the suffering, the problem of how to change human nature and selfishness remains the greatest problem of all. As fast as one desperate situation is helped, new and still more widespread sufferings break forth, simply because a solution to the problem of self-centeredness has not been found, and as long as it exists it creates evil conditions continually. It is impossible to force men to be good by punishing them for selfishness and wrongs against their fellowmen, or even by forcibly depriving them of the power to do evil.

Evil can only be abolished by awakening in the hearts of men and women a passionate desire for goodness, and this is exactly what Jesus did. He exemplified the only successful way of dealing with evil: "overcome evil with good" (Romans 12:21). Replace the desire to act selfishly with a passionate desire to act for the benefit of all. Here is Christ's revolutionary message, given in Matthew 5:44, 45: "I say unto you, Love your enemies, bless them that curse you, do good to them that hate you, and pray for them which despitefully use you, and persecute you; that ye may be the children of your Father which is in heaven: for he maketh his sun to rise on the evil and on the good, and sendeth rain on the just and on the unjust."

"But it's utterly impossible to do that and it won't work," people tell me.

But it does work, and Jesus triumphantly

demonstrated that it did.

We have already looked at Jesus' methods in fighting evil, but just a few more words are needed here.

The country where Jesus lived had been invaded and conquered by a terribly cruel world power—Rome. He lived and carried on his ministry in an enemy-occupied country where brutal and hardened Roman legionaries continually committed the most appalling atrocities, such as public crucifixions (the most agonizingly painful death ever invented) of any who dared to join secret resistance movements or to protest the policies of Rome and Caesar. Public floggings of the most brutal kind for even small offenses were commonplace. Slavery was practiced on a scale never known before, and death by stoning was permitted for infringements of the religious laws of the country.

How did Jesus react to this situation and what did he teach his followers to do under these dreadful conditions? What method did he advocate for combatting such evils as these? Did he urge his followers to join underground resistance movements, or exhort them courageously to denounce in public the appalling injustices and cruelties and horrible practices such as slavery, and willingly to undergo a martyr's death as a result, and encourage others to do likewise? Did he perhaps organize peaceful protest marches and send petitions to the Roman authorities on behalf of the wrong and suffering?

No, he did not! There is not a single suggestion anywhere in the New Testament that Jesus ever advocated or supported any such methods as these. There is not a single hint that he ever protested to the authorities against the atrocities and evil practices of the Roman legionaries, or that he ever uttered a word of condemnation against the policies of the conquerors of his nation. There is not a single instance of his denouncing either Herod, the puppet king appointed by the Romans (as John the Baptist did), or Pilate, the Roman governor, or Caiaphas, the politically minded high priest at that time. He never spoke a word against Caesar, the head of that vast empire composed of millions of slaves in conquered nations, ruled by a small minority of rich and powerful Roman citizens who had complete control over all the others. Those citizens lived lives of selfish luxury and entertained themselves with diabolically cruel public sports, watching men kill each other or be torn to pieces by wild beasts.

Jesus said absolutely nothing about all this. Didn't he care? Why did he remain silent and do nothing? Why didn't he use his miraculous powers to destroy the Roman conquerors and free his country? Was it not because he knew that to use miraculous powers destructively would only make matters far, far worse, and that there is only one really successful way of overcoming evil and rescuing people from the evils in which they have become imprisoned? He knew that any empire founded on destructive force and unchecked selfishness and cruelty is doomed. He knew the Roman Empire was already crumbling and about to collapse. He also knew that even when that happened, if evil were left undealt with in the right way, it would only spring up again under another and even more dreadful form. So he set about a rescue mission which would use completely different and God-inspired means, and thus would demonstrate the only successful way of overcoming evil.

His method? Modeling righteousness, living in godliness so others would want the same kind of life, seeing its tremendous superiority to selfishness.

As we imitate Christ in being examples of unselfish, meaningful living, we must constantly guard against being polluted by the evil world in which for a time we must live. We must practice separation from everything which breaks the royal law of love, separation from all "love of the world," separation from everything which causes us to stumble and to be in bondage to our "besetting sins," whatever they may be. In a word, it is separation from everything that blunts our taste for heavenly things. For it is only by complete separation from such things that we can develop new tastes and be able to enjoy and appreciate all the delights of heaven; which delights, to "the natural man," appear insipid, boring, tasteless.

How many of us Christians remain sadly unable to enjoy spiritual pleasures because we keep trying to satisfy our worldly appetites? We foster our worldly ambitions, gorge ourselves with worldly pleasures (not the gross ones which many non-Christians indulge in, but worldly in the sense that they keep us thinking or valuing or reacting the same way the world does).

In this matter no two of us are just alike. But if certain kinds of books, music, recreation, or television shows absorb more time than we feel comfortable about, or if they make spiritual things seem insipid to us afterward, then at least for a time let us cut them out of our lives. If certain pleasures, innocent in themselves and quite harmless for others, make us feel restless and dissatisfied with spiritual pleasures afterward, then let us not waste time on those things, for they will blunt our spiritual taste and finally destroy it altogether. That is why the Scriptures are so full of challenges to separation.

Let us never, however, distort the meaning of separation by supposing that we must separate from other Christians with whom we do not agree, or who do not believe as we do and have erroneous ideas! It may indeed be well to keep separate from discussions on those matters on which we disagree, if such discussions unsettle our peace, and more especially if they stir us up to angry argument and irritated feelings. Nothing will kill the taste for heavenly things quicker than a habit of despising and condemning other members of the body of Christ and disowning them! That habit will make the real heaven most distasteful to us—for so many will be there in it whom we think ought not to be there and whom we have refused to love and accept.

Real worldliness (that is, setting too high a value on the temporary passing things in the world of sense) will deaden our spiritual tastes more than anything else. A passionate desire to be "in fashion," to be just like everybody else, to have what others have, to adopt the standards of one's fellow church members (even if those standards are obviously far below and contradictory to the standard of Christ as he taught it in the Sermon on the Mount), snobbishness, exclusiveness, setting a high value on popularity, position, or profit, coveting publicity—these are all things which most effectively prevent the development of this vital taste for spiritual things, without which we cannot possibly enjoy, or even desire, godliness. Such tastes cause us to desire an imaginary heaven of our own creating, containing the sort of pleasures which we really do enjoy—the pleasures of high position, preeminence, and human glory. Such a heaven might even prove to be a kind of hell!

A corollary of separation involves relinquishing earthly riches or possessions, being willing to give them up, not calling them our own. We must be willing to let everything go at the right time, as the trees so beautifully let go of all their leafy treasures, allowing them to drop off, sealing over the vacant spot so that not a pang of loss remains. We must let them go as sweetly as an elderly friend of mine was preparing to do as she was about to be uprooted from her beloved little home and to be transplanted to a strange new environment (a nursing home) where there would be no room for her old treasures. We should want to loosen our roots from earthly things, in order to put them down more and more strongly in the higher heavenly world hidden beyond the veil of our physical sight. We should begin now to make that world more real to our inner consciousness than this earthly one is to our bodily senses.

This world in which we now walk is a dying world. Death is a constant part of this world.

But there can be no real "death" for the Christian. The discarding of his physical body is like putting off an outer garment not needed as soon as one arrives home! For citizens of the Kingdom there will be no loss of consciousness, for when, like an ebbing tide, the consciousness ebbs away from the physical and material realm, it simply flows into another channel altogether, namely into the spiritual world, and becomes the radiant consciousness of coming into the welcome and love of the Father's house.

As a result of early teaching I retained the idea for a very long time that the souls of Christians, as well as the souls of all others, remain after death in a state of unconsciousness which can be likened to sleep, and from that sleep they will be wakened at "the last trump," only then to begin a resurrection life either of blessedness in heaven or of torment and despair in endless separation from God. But surely such an idea is a misunderstanding of the beautiful metaphor used by the Lord when he said, "Our friend Lazarus sleepeth, but I go, that I may awake him out of sleep." This metaphor was taken over by the early Christians who always described death as "falling asleep" in the Lord. What can this mean but the lovely, best way of expressing the wonderful truth that death is nothing but falling asleep to the physical and material world (just as we do every time we fall asleep at night) and not waking again to the physical consciousness to which we have always before returned, but awaking to the spiritual world instead.

That this is true seems to be clearly confirmed by the description of Stephen's death (Acts 7:55, 56): "He looked up steadfastly into heaven, and saw the glory of God, and Jesus standing on the right hand of God, and said, Behold, I see the heavens opened, and the Son of man standing on the right hand of God."

Someone has pointed out that this is the only occasion on which the Lord is described as standing, and not sitting, on the right hand of God, as though it is thus beautifully suggested to us that the Lord had sprung to his feet to welcome his first martyr witness! But what a terrible anti-climax if, a moment later, when it says (v. 60), "And when he had said this, he fell asleep" it means that at that moment his spirit as well as his body became unconscious, and he thus missed the whole welcome!

No, when the Lord said, "Our friend Lazarus sleepeth, but I go, that I may awake him out of sleep," he meant that he would awaken him once again to physical consciousness. And when he also said, "He that believeth on me shall never die," he was stating the glorious fact for our comfort and cheer that we who believe on him will never experience death in any way except as a loss of physical consciousness.

Nowadays there seems to be a conspiracy of silence on this subject, as though the very idea of thinking happily about our real homeland or "the world to come" while we are still in this one is in some way unseemly and morbid.

We are told that in olden times (I don't know if the practice is still continued) the monks in very strict Carmelite orders slept each night in their coffins and kept a skull in each cell, so that they could in this way familiarize themselves with the thought of death and with the fleeting temporality of this life.

It is easy to call such a custom a morbid and unhealthy preoccupation with death. But I really wonder if it is any more morbid and unhealthy than refusing altogether to think about the future hour of our departure from this world, or to talk to one another about dying. Why do we refuse to familiarize ourselves with the wonderful and inescapable event with which each one of us will be confronted sometime—our departure from this world into the next—the putting off of these mortal, physical bodies in order to put on our new, immortal, heavenly bodies, so that we may enter rejoicingly into an incomparably richer form of life in a higher, heavenly world.

Surely it is a strange, morbid, and unhealthy thing to be afraid to mention death to the dying; to make it the "unmentionable subject" which it has become. The early Christians, constantly persecuted and confronted by the threat of death, adopted quite a different attitude toward it. Instead of seeking to escape from all thoughts about it, they confronted it bravely and looked it full in the face and saw it for what it really is, an old scarecrow, a defeated foe, a nothing dressed up as though it were something terrible. For them, the death and resurrection of Jesus had unveiled the glorious truth that death has been swallowed up in victory. It's not what men have fearfully thought it to be, at least not for the child of God. It is simply the physical process of putting off an outworn mortal garment in order to put on a new immortal one in which to pass over into the real world, compared to which this world is like a bad dream.

So the early Christians familiarized themselves with the idea of death. They talked about it together and sang about it most joyfully and made hopeful preparations, so that however suddenly and unexpectedly it might come, they would be ready to take their departure, with everything left well arranged and as easy as possible to deal with for those who were left behind. Their loved ones were constantly being carried off to prison, and then violently deprived of their physical bodies, and no one knew when his own turn would come. That's why they learned to confront the idea joyfully and hopefully and to prepare for it gladly. That was why they so exulted in the resurrection of Jesus, for it was glorious proof that death really is only a door into the higher world, rather like another birth out of the womb of this earth into the world of heaven. So the idea of passing over became as familiar and joyful an idea to them as is the prospect of returning home for the holidays to the student at college. How strange and sad that in our day and generation, this attitude seems to be so altered.

Like Bunyan's Pilgrim, I myself want to let "my thoughts wax warm about where I am going," and like countless pilgrims before me, make secret, happy plans for the glorious coming change and my arrival in my real homeland.

"Now before the feast of the passover, when Jesus knew that his hour was come, that he should depart out of this world unto the Father, having loved his own which were in the world, he loved them unto the end" (John 13:1).

"His hour was come" (as it will come, someday, to each one of us), that he should depart out of this world. How did he prepare for it? Why, just at this particular point, does it say these beautiful words—"Having loved his own which were in the world, he loved them unto the end"?

He well knew that his departure from this world would be through the door of an agonizing death, hanging for hours on a cross, experiencing the most terrible form of death that fallen human beings have ever invented. Yet he didn't spend his last hours thinking about himself. He devoted himself to thinking lovingly and compassionately about his friends and their needs, and picturing the best way to help those who, not realizing it, were so soon to be bereaved of the heavenly joy and assurance and security of his physical presence. This continued "unto the end"—even when he was hanging on the cross. Strong and serene, and even joyful in this redemptive ministry of love, he was assured that when the hour came, he would be succoured and brought through in triumph.

Unlike him, we fear death. It has become an "unmentionable subject," so fearful an idea that human beings do not like to speak about it to each other. So many of us are terrified at the thought of the suffering that may precede it, the long, lingering illness—cancer, a stroke, paralysis, complete helplessness, blindness, deafness, failing strength, unbearable pain. The Bible is very tender and understanding on this subject. It speaks compassionately of those "who through fear of death were all their lifetime subject to bondage" (Hebrews 2:15) and promises that we can be delivered from that fear by the Lord who "through death" destroyed "him that had the power of death" (v. 14). I myself, for a long time, was very much afraid of dying. Like many others who possess a vivid imagination, I was tempted to picture to myself the whole process of lingering disease and death, and to shrink in terror from it.

I well remember the occasion years ago when a middle-aged woman came to me after I had been speaking at a meeting and said to me in a trembling voice, as she caught hold of my hands, "Hannah, I have cancer, and the doctors say that they cannot operate. I am simply terrified. There is such a little time left. Can no one do anything to help me and to keep me alive?"

A pang went right through my own heart. I could picture and feel exactly how she felt, just how I would be feeling myself if I were in her place. I could only put my arms around her and say with tears of compassion, "Oh, I really am certain that when you reach the time you so much dread, you will find the loving Lord and Savior there, waiting to help you and to carry you right through in triumph, and without fear. He will not fail you if you cast yourself upon him and seek his help. Once I too had to have an operation (though not for cancer), and I was dreadfully afraid until I reached the operating room, and then—there he was, and all the fear went, swallowed up in peace. I am sure it will be the same for you, because you see, he loves us and delights in helping us if we will give him the opportunity to do so." Then I told her about an old friend of my mother's who, many years ago, was dying with cancer.

She sent a message asking me to go and see her. I was only a very young Christian and was dreadfully afraid of seeing pain, and I shrank from going. But when I entered her room I saw her lying on the bed (almost at the end of the journey), and her face was simply radiant. She did not speak to me about herself at all, but only asked for news about myself and the other members of the family. I was only allowed to stay for a few minutes, and then the nurse beckoned me from the room. But there was one question I simply had to ask before I left—never to see her again. "They tell me that you are nearly always in great pain. Please, please, will you tell me how you bear it, for I am so dreadfully afraid of pain myself."

Her face lit up. "So was I," she said. "I have always been afraid of dying because of the pain that might precede it. I feared that the pain would be so great that it would make it impossible for me to realize the presence of my Lord, and that I should be crazed by it. I was afraid that even he would not be able to keep me in peace and joy and contact with himself in the fires of suffering. But, Hannah, it has all been so different from what I feared and imagined. For never in all my life before has his presence been so real to me, or his peace and joy so great as now. I am truly glad that he let me come this way, because I could never have known how wonderful he is and how absolutely sufficient his grace can be."

Then she asked me to pick up the Bible which was lying open on the table beside her, and to read the verse which was underlined on that page. I did so and read these words. "Beloved, think it not strange concerning the fiery trial which is to try you, as though some strange thing happened unto you: but rejoice, inasmuch as ye are partakers of Christ's sufferings; that when his glory shall be revealed, ye shall be glad also with exceeding joy" (1 Peter 4:12).

My friend went on, "Those words have returned to me again and again. They formed, indeed, the first step on the pathway of escape from my own fear of death and pain. They helped me to believe that no matter how I may feel beforehand, when I get to the situation I have so much dreaded and may have been tempted to picture with fear and dismay, I shall find that he really is there, ready to bear me safely through. He has never been known to fail the weak and the fearful who seek his aid. How I love the words which John Bunyan put into the mouth of Mr. Great-Heart when he was describing the journey of Mr. Fearing to the Celestial City. Mr. Fearing, he tells us, was all through his journey terrified by everything he pictured and supposed would happen to him, especially as he drew near to the River which had to be crossed before the City could be reached. He was certain that he would be lost forever in the River and never reach the goal of his heart's desire. 'But our Lord is of very tender compassions towards them that are afraid,' said Mr. Great-Heart, 'and I took note that when Mr. Fearing entered the river, it was at lower ebb than I ever saw it before or since, so he crossed over, almost dry-shod.' "

Isn't that lovely! Indeed our Lord has tender compassion for them that are afraid. I know this from my own experience—

again and again. I have found it true that he does not despise us for our fears. He does not add to them by chidingly warning us that we bring upon ourselves the very things we fear. Absolutely not. He knows that without him we cannot pull ourselves together and escape from the clutches of our fears. He understands perfectly, and he succours us. From my own oft repeated experiences of his grace and tender help, I can testify that "better hath he been for years, than my fears!" Again and again I have exclaimed with thankful, exulting joy, "This is the 'tomorrow' that I so much dreaded—and it hasn't happened! Praise him!"

I think another thing about death and "the hour of departure from this world" that we are tempted to dread is the fact that we are not sure what lies beyond death. When we put off these mortal bodies, it means that we pass beyond the reach of everything familiar, out into an unknown world—and the unknown terrifies some of us very much indeed.

A little while ago a friend was telling some of us about her grandfather's death. For some reason, almost till the end of his illness, he was filled with fear and dread. At last he even struggled up in the bed, crying out and begging those who were present to keep him from dying. Then suddenly he looked up, his face changed, and he exclaimed, "Oh, if it's like that, I want to go!"

Then he lay back peacefully in the bed and went.

When the veil of our physical senses tears apart and the real world begins to appear before us, how glorious it will be!

> When death these mortal eyes shall seal
> And still this throbbing heart,
> The rending veil shall thee reveal,
> All glorious as thou art.

Someday a wonderful thing is going to happen to me, something like that described in the Song of Songs. I shall find myself saying, "I sleep, but my heart waketh; it is the voice of my Beloved that knocketh, saying, Open to me." No, it will not be death knocking at the door of my heart, for there is no death; it has been swallowed up in victory. It will be the Eternal Life himself, my Lord, my heart's beloved. Into his arms I shall fling myself and go with him into our Father's world.

Let us encourage one another with this glorious hope, and follow the example of that dear Lord who knew "that his hour was come, that he should depart out of this world unto the Father, having loved his own which were in the world, he loved them unto the end" (John 13:1). Yes, let us concentrate on this glorious ministry of forgetting self and loving others, and then when the River is actually reached, we too shall find that we are taken through it "dry-shod." For has not our dear Lord said, "Whosoever ... believeth on me shall never die ... he shall never see death" (John 11:26; 8:51).

CHAPTER 5
Kingdom Living

Citizenship in the Kingdom of God comes by faith in Jesus Christ. Once in the Kingdom, how are we to live? What does God expect of us?

The Lord summed up principles of heavenly living in the Beatitudes (Matthew 5:3-12). The rest of the Sermon on the Mount (Matthew 5:13—7:29) is a summary of the lessons which the Lord taught his disciples about these principles.

"Blessed" or "happy" are those who practice these heavenly principles and who allow God's power to work in them. Without that power it is impossible to live the Beatitudes.

The Poor in Spirit

"Blessed are the poor in spirit: for theirs is the kingdom of heaven" (Matthew 5:3).

This first heavenly principle is enlarged upon in 6:24—"No man can serve two masters ... ye cannot serve God and mammon."

The word used for poor is a word meaning beggary and refers to one who owns nothing at all but must receive everything from others.

All the Lord's sayings, when earnestly and honestly considered, are like dynamite! They blow to pieces men's usual standards and ideas about life. This one is no exception. It is terrific! It is the foundation principle of the Kingdom of heaven. Indeed, the Lord speaks of this first heavenly principle as though it alone puts anyone in the Kingdom of heaven and gives him the right to be a citizen. "Theirs is the kingdom of heaven."

But is not the Lord Jesus Christ himself, according to his own words, the door into the Kingdom of heaven, and faith in him the only way in?

Yes, indeed, and this first Beatitude simply confirms it.

The way, the one way, to enter into the Kingdom of heaven is to come to the Lord and lay down at his feet everything we are, and every single thing we possess, to give up our right of ownership entirely and irrevocably. To be poor in spirit is to stop ruling ourselves and submit to him. Just as the camels which were to pass in through a specially narrow gate of Jerusalem—so narrow it was named "the eye of a needle"—had to unlade every single thing before they could pass through, so anyone who wishes to enter the Kingdom of heaven comes to the door of heaven, Christ himself, and surrenders every single thing to him. It is the most drastic experience in a man's life. No wonder the Lord spoke of it in these terms: "Strive [agonize] to enter in at the strait gate." It is an agonizing experience, for it means such faith in Jesus Christ and such obedient response to his challenge and command that we surrender every single thing we call our own—possessions, rights, time, talents, loved ones—everything. It is the signing away of all we possess, making it all over to the Lord. "No man can serve two masters," and just as no man can serve God and wealth, so no man can make Christ and self master at the same time.

Granted, none of us can surrender everything to God all at once. But at the moment we invite Christ into our lives, we begin to do so. Day after day he helps us to "build altars" and surrender the unheavenly things he brings to our attention. As God's children, the overall pattern of our lives should be an attitude of poverty.

Blessed are those who reduce themselves to beggary "in spirit," i.e., with all their will and heart, who sign away their rights of possession to the Lord himself; for theirs is the right to be citizens of the Kingdom of heaven. "Sell all that thou hast and follow me," said the Lord to the rich young ruler who had great possessions.

There is no escape from this principle, which seems so appalling and impossible to the man who is not in touch with God. How many, like the rich young ruler, have gone away sorrowful when they have heard the terms upon which alone they can enter the Kingdom of heaven? How many have cried out, "But the gospel says salvation is a 'gift of God' and not to be bought at all! It is all of mercy and grace! How, then, can it possibly be claimed that heaven and the right of heavenly citizenship must be bought with such a price as this?"

Ah yes, mercy and grace and forgiveness are free—free as the air. But the right to enter the Kingdom of heaven goes only to those who bow before Jesus Christ, who is the way in.

In the fourteenth century, St. Francis of Assisi taught his followers that a citizen of heaven owns nothing at all. Everything he uses is lent him by the real owner, his Lord and Master, and the moment his Lord says someone else is now to use what has been lent to him, he joyfully yields it up at once—for it never was his, but only lent for his use as long as needed.

This, and this alone, is true faith in Christ—this uttermost surrender to him. Everything passes out of our possession into his. There are some to whom he may give the personal command "Sell all that thou hast and give to the poor" because (as in the individual case of the rich young ruler) wealth, and the power bestowed on them by that wealth, were ruining them. They could not keep it even as a loan from God, because it had already snared them into slavery. To others he says, Retain these things you have hitherto possessed, but only as a loan from myself and to be used as I direct, not in the way you have hitherto been using them. That is his affair.

To some he may not say, "Give away everything you possess" but rather, "Cast away your reputation, everything you have built up through the years." Or, "Cast away that job and begin this other kind of work which I have chosen for you." Or, "Cast away those needless luxuries, that spending on yourself and your family the money I need for other purposes."

Whatever it is, it may be the one thing which we feel it is most impossible to give up. It is the things which we so specially love and cleave to which are the idols of our heart and are rivals in our love and surrender to him. It is the rival master which he will insist on dethroning first of all. And then, year by year, day by day, we shall live constantly yielding whatever he asks of us and thereby discover that "ours is the Kingdom of heaven."

If God asks you to literally give away what you have, beware of making a public display of it. The Pharisees and scribes made a great show of this; they advertised their gifts to God's work and to the Temple ministry. Indeed, if they gave a sufficiently large gift to the Temple treasury, a trumpet was blown to announce the fact to everyone. There are so many unworthy motives, even for giving "the Lord's money" (for all is his) for special purposes. The motive for it may be that we have heard that "God is never in any man's debt" and pays back with compound interest all that is given to his work. I have met not a few who were painfully disappointed over the results of their giving because it left them almost in penury, sometimes even in debt and borrowing from the bank or from friends; while other givers (especially secret ones) did seem to receive, almost incredibly, "royal dividends." It all depends upon the motives which lead to such tithing and "giving to the Lord," and those motives can be mixed and selfish.

There may be the secret (perhaps unrecognized) temptation to give generous gifts in order to buy friendship, or even power over others, the right to "act Providence" in the lives of those who depend on such gifts, the right to dictate to others, or to win a place of influence on a committee, or simply and solely to win applause and a reputation for being generous to the Lord's work. Then, too, like the Pharisees of old, we need to remember the solemn warning of the Lord that nothing must be given to "the Lord's work" which is really needed for the relief and support of aged parents or helpless dependents. Heavenly love must feel that supplying the needs of those really dependent upon us, because they cannot work for themselves, is just as much God's work as sending missionaries to the foreign field or helping to build a new church. All is God's work which is done under the control of the Holy Spirit. Perhaps some of us need to reread the Lord's words in Mark 7:11, 12, when he spoke about "Corban." Corban simply means a gift paid into the Temple treasury to be used for maintaining the Temple services. The Lord said that no such gifts should be given to the Temple if the giver's own parents needed financial help instead.

There is no risk in giving to God. The Lord to whom we have surrendered everything will see to it that everything necessary for the work to which he has called us is abundantly and continuously supplied.

The poor in spirit humble themselves, considering all they possess to be God's, trusting him to care for all their needs. This is a life of dependence on God, a life of faith.

FAITH

Faith is response to Love's dear call,
  Of Love's own face the sight!
To do Love's bidding now is all
  That gives the heart delight.
To love thy voice and to reply,
  "Lord, here am I!"

As blows the wind through summer trees
  Till all the leaves are stirred,
O Spirit move as thou dost please,
  My heart yields at thy word;
Faith hears Thee calling from beyond—
  And doth respond.

What thou dost will—that I desire,
  Through me let it be done;
Thy will and mine in Love's own fire
  Are welded into one.
"Lord, I believe!" Nay, rather say,
  "Lord, I obey!"

The Sorrowful

"Blessed are they that mourn: for they shall be comforted" (Matthew 5:4). This principle is also enlarged in 6:25-34, when the Lord pointed to the birds and the flowers of the field who have no anxious, troubled thoughts and never bewail their lot or circumstances, and know nothing of self-pity and crushing despair or bitterness when overtaken by disaster. It is the lovely, heavenly principle of believing that "your heavenly Father knoweth that ye have need of all these things," even though everything we cherish is swept away from us, and of believing that our sorrow will all be turned to joy.

In this second heavenly principle our Lord gives what can really be described as a plain statement which completely contradicts everything we men and women take for granted. He affirms that mourning reacted to aright will bring joy, and therefore things that cause ordinary men of the world to wail and lament are really blessings in disguise.

The heavenly attitude toward sorrow and grief and all experiences of suffering in this world is in total contrast to the natural attitude we know so well. Our Lord was "acquainted with grief" and suffering, and caused great good to come out of it. Not that we are to seek these things, but we are never to fear them. We should rather use them. God, who so loves us that he allows us, like his own dear Son, to learn obedience by the things that we suffer (Hebrews 5:8), wants us to use them creatively. There would be no suffering and no sorrow permitted to God's children unless all such experiences were, in actual fact, a means to heavenly and eternal blessing which could not otherwise be ours.

Henry Suso, writing in the Middle Ages in *The Little Book of Eternal Wisdom,* made some of the most beautiful and wonderful comments on this second heavenly principle that I have ever read. He tells us that he heard Eternal Love saying: "'I cannot endure that the soul should fall back upon aught else but myself, with joy and pleasure, so I block up all roads with thorns; I stop up all gaps with hardships, and, lest it should escape me, I strew its way with suffering.' ... There is nothing more painful than suffering and nothing more joyful than to have suffered... A man who has not suffered, what does he know? ... Suffering keeps the soul humble, teaches patience; it is a guardian of purity and brings the crown of eternal bliss. There can scarcely be a man who does not receive some good from suffering ... All the saints are the cupbearers of a suffering man, for they have all tasted it once themselves and they cry out with one voice that it is a wholesome cup and free from poison."

This is the "cup" which the Lord himself drank in the Garden of Gethsemane when he cried out, "Not my will, but thine be done."

The Greek word translated "mourn" is not the word for sorrow or suffering, but it is a word meaning to lament, to be sad, to bewail. That is to say, it refers to the experience of enduring suffering, sorrow, tribulation, etc., and our Lord declares that, in the Kingdom of heaven, all who experience this are blessed. Then he gives the reason why this is so: "For they shall be comforted." And the word he used for "comforted" is the same word used in the New Testament for the Paraclete or Comforter, the Holy

Spirit himself, "One called alongside to help."

It is in times of sorrow and tribulation and suffering when we call on the Comforter and draw nearer to God, simply because we cannot, and dare not, be left alone! Looking back over their lives, everyone in the Kingdom of heaven knows that all the richest and best and loveliest and most enriching things have come to them through sorrows and griefs; through circumstances which caused the heart to break; through experiences of loss which seemed as though they would be overwhelming. Even as I write and think back over my own pathway of life, I know beyond a shadow of doubt that all the best treasures and blessings have come to me while I was obliged to keep company with sorrow and suffering. There was no poison in the cup at all.

There can be poison in the cup of sorrow, however—but only if we put it there ourselves by reacting to these mournful circumstances with self-pity, resentment, and angry struggles to evade the cup instead of drinking it! It all depends upon how we react to the things which make us mourn. We can react in the heavenly way, receiving them in the sure knowledge that they are to bring us greater enrichment and that all our sorrow will be turned into joy. And, therefore, there is only one thing to do: to call upon the Comforter and lay ourselves down in his hands in perfect submission and childlike trust. Struggling to evade the things that grieve and bereave us; passionately clinging to the idols of our hearts when they are being forced from us; bitter resentment that such things should be allowed to happen—these are the earthly and not the heavenly reactions, and they will poison the cup and make it almost impossible to drink.

"My brethren, count it all joy when ye fall into divers temptations [trials]" (James 1:2). If we react to difficult situations with trust in God, difficult, unlovely, overwhelming, and disastrous things will bring praise and glory to God forever. Out of all our testing circumstances, by reacting to them in the heavenly way, we produce heavenly treasures. We have a lovely example of this in the material world, for all the really precious jewels, such as the diamond and ruby, are formed under immense and terrible pressure or by fiercest heat!

In ages past, men sought to find the secret of "the philosopher's stone," by means of which everything could be transmuted into pure gold. Christ has taught us the real secret for transforming earthly and temporary experiences into eternal treasure. It is this principle of sorrow rightly received, with joyful trust and glad submission, grief used as God desires it to be used. It is tragic that so many Christians do not practice the principle, and so do not fully experience the joy of the Lord. But all those who do can echo the Psalmist's words out of a heart full of joy and thankfulness: "We went through fire and through water: but thou broughtest us out into a wealthy place" (Psalm 66:12). Think of what it means to let God bring good out of evil and blessing out of sadness.

No matter what circumstances come our way, we can have confidence and hope.

JOY

Hark to Love's triumphant shout!
    Joy is born from pain;
Joy is sorrow inside out;
    Grief remade again.
Broken hearts, look up and see,
This is Love's own victory.

Here marred things are made anew,
    Filth is here made clean;
Here are robes, not rags for you,
    Mirth where tears have been.
Where sin's dreadful power was found,
Grace doth now much more abound!

Hark! such songs of jubilation,
    Every creature sings!
Great the joy of every nation,
    Love is King of kings.
See, ye blind ones! shout ye dumb!
Joy is sorrow overcome.

The Meek

"Blessed are the meek: for they shall inherit the earth" (Matthew 5:5). The Greek word here means "mild, gentle, kind, meek, forbearing." It is the exact opposite of self-assertion and self-will. Our Lord describes it more fully in 5:38-41, where we find that it is the principle of no tit for tat, no reprisals. At the same time it is not passive but active resistance—employing another kind of power altogether, God's power which comes to us as we joyfully accept everything which is allowed to happen to us. The heavenly way of dealing with evildoers who wrong us personally is "Resist not evil [with force]: but whosoever shall smite thee on thy right cheek, turn to him the other also." Not that we are to take this always in a completely literal sense, for experience shows that it can be an irresistible temptation to some to have another cheek offered to them, and may, indeed, aggravate the offense. Jesus meant we are not to assert ourselves, but rather to be willing to suffer loss if it will help the wrongdoer. To give to a hypocritical and lazy person is not the way to help him. It is really cruel to give money to some weak and habit-bound people who cannot help themselves but must hurry to the nearest bar or restaurant for a drink. Our Lord was speaking from the point of view of the citizen of heaven, not from the point of view of the wrongdoer. He does not encourage us to give to thieves more than they have already stolen, or to encourage those who practice violence. But he does teach a principle which can help the evildoer and change him completely.

The New Testament urges us to pray for those in authority, those who punish evildoers and enforce justice. "Rulers are not a terror to good works, but to the evil ... for he is the minister of God to thee for good. But if thou do that which is evil, be afraid; for he beareth not the sword in vain: for he is the minister of God, a revenger to execute wrath upon him that doeth evil" (Romans 13:3, 4). In the world, at present, governments and police forces are necessary, but for those in the Kingdom of heaven there is a far more satisfactory principle for them to practice and a far mightier power than force for them to exercise. It is the principle of active gentleness and kindness and forbearance (with wisdom and understanding). It is not a principle which allows evildoers to get away with their ill-gotten gains, but rather of gentle and wise understanding of why they so acted, and willingness to give the right kind of help to them in their need, even if it means loss to ourselves. And this wisdom and power to help them can only come by practicing meekness.

MEEKNESS

O blessed are the patient meek
    Who quietly suffer wrong;
How glorious are the "foolish weak"
    By God made greatly strong;
So strong they take the conqueror's crown,
And turn the whole world upside down.

O dreaded meek! None can resist
   The weapon which they wield;
Force melts before them like a mist,
   Earth's strong men faint and yield.
Yes, slay the meek—lay them in dust,
But bow before them earth's might must!

Immortal meek! They take the earth
   By flinging all away;
They die—and death is but their birth,
   They lose—and win the day.
Hewn down and stripped and scorned and slain,
As earth's true kings they rise and reign!

O Christlike meek! by heaven blessed,
   Before whom hell must quake!
By foolish, blinded men oppressed,
   The earth itself they take.
O seed of him who won through loss,
And conquered death while on a cross!

The Hungry

"Blessed are they which do hunger and thirst after righteousness: for they shall be filled" (Matthew 5:6).

This principle is cousin to 5:27-32, where the Lord refers to lust and warns us to "cut off" completely from our lives everything which snares us into misusing sexual instincts and directing them into immoral channels. "If thy right eye offend thee, pluck it out, and cast it from thee ... if thy right hand offend thee, cut it off, and cast it from thee."

The Greek word translated "hunger" means "to be famished," and, metaphorically speaking, "to hunger after or desire earnestly." The word for "thirst," used metaphorically, means "to long for ardently." Both words used by the Lord refer to a hunger and thirst of the heart and soul.

Not until I lived in Palestine did I know anything about the strength of physical thirst and the way in which, as it increases, it makes it impossible to think of anything else. During my first summer in that country, I went with a party of other missionaries on a donkey ride into the wilderness of Judea, to visit the remote and famous ancient monastery of Mar Saba. It was midday in August when we started off on this four-hour ride through the bare, treeless desert, and when at last we reached the monastery, we were unable to think of anything but a passionate desire to drink. A monk led us into the guest room, in the floor of which was a deep well. By means of long cords, two cups were let down into the well, and clear, cold water drawn up. In turn we each drank about twenty cups of the water for which every part of our bodies was so urgently craving. The soul or spirit of man is capable of thirst equally intense— the thirst for acceptance by God and for all the good things of which he is the author.

The need, so strong in every normal human being, for love is a hunger and thirst implanted by the Creator himself. That it is, perhaps, the strongest instinct of all seems clearly confirmed by the fact that the daily papers, magazines, movies, and books of today so largely concentrate on the theme of this universal craving. That for multitudes of men and women it remains an unsatisfied and frustrated instinct also seems clear, for we are constantly having our attention drawn to examples of misuse, distortion, abuse, and crime resulting from the fact that satisfaction has been sought in all sorts of wrong, useless, and mistaken ways. To countless multitudes this instinct and capacity for love has become a torment and a tyrant, instead of the wonderful and glorious thing which the Creator purposed, the means whereby the sons and daughters of God are to be made creative on the highest possible level.

Our Lord taught that this strongest and highest of our instincts and capacities, if it results in faith in him, will be abundantly satisfied and will generate a joy of living that nothing else can produce.

He described this desire for love and union with God as a hunger and thirst, or passionate desire, after righteousness and said that on that level, it will be completely satisfied.

Now righteousness is everything that is right, like God, in harmony with his universal law of love. We know what God is like because we have seen "the express image of his person" manifested to us in the Lord Jesus Christ (Hebrews 1:3). "Christ Jesus ..." wrote the Apostle Paul, "is made unto us ...

104

righteousness" (1 Corinthians 1:30). He is the perfect pattern of righteousness—he is Righteousness personified, the expression of everything that is right and lovely and like God. Therefore, to become Christ-centered, to turn the whole force of this mighty instinct of love upon him, to direct all the desire and longings of the heart toward him is the one, sure way to satisfy this hunger and thirst for love and union on the spiritual level. And union with God is possible only by believing in Jesus Christ as Savior and personal Lord. He then credits all his righteousness to our spiritual account.

It is, of course, in perfect harmony with God's plan for men and women that they should seek love and union in marriage and so satisfy this instinct for love and creativity in the way which God has himself appointed. When it is "marriage in the Lord," unity in love to him as well as to each other, it reaches its highest perfection on the earthly level. But it is often forgotten that this love instinct must also be satisfied on a higher level, and until this is the case, one cannot know true and full satisfaction and fulfillment. Our Creator has so fashioned us that for both unmarried and married people this hunger and thirst can never be fully satisfied except through union with Christ himself. Saint Augustine summed it up when he told us that God made us for himself and our hearts can never find true rest until we find it in him.

Francis Thomson also expressed this truth that even the most perfect human marriage cannot fully satisfy this God-created hunger and thirst:

The sweetest wife on sweetest marriage day...
Sweet to her sweet may say:
"I take you to my inmost heart, my true!"
Ah, fool! but there is one heart you
Shall never take him to!
The hold that falls not when the town is got,
The heart's heart, whose immured plot
Hath keys yourself keep not;...
Its keys are at the cincture hung of God;
Its gates are trepidant to His nod;
By Him its floors are trod.

Yes, the inmost abyss or heart of hearts in every human being is so shaped that none but the Creator can wholly fill it.

When this truth is realized, then even the most lonely and thwarted person can find perfect fulfillment and creative satisfaction through the love of Christ. This can only be brought about through the habit of continually laying down our own wills and desires and thrusting them down deeply into the will and desires of Christ, or as he himself expressed it, by abiding in the vine as the branches do, and yielding to the life of the vine.

When we live this kind of a life, our hunger is satisfied and we become channels

for the reproduction of the life of God in
others.

UNION

My bonds are very, very strong,
   I never can go free;
To holy Love I now belong,
   And he belongs to me.
And all the power of earth and heaven
Into my Love-chained hands are given.

Controlled by him I have no might
   To let self plan or choose;
But this control is my delight,
   And freedom I refuse.
The King of love as Lord I own,
And sit with him upon his throne.

Creative power! O perfect joy,
   O union made complete!
This life, death never can destroy,
   Nor this fruition sweet.
Each member of the Church, his Bride,
Christ-centered—and so satisfied.

The Merciful

"Blessed are the merciful: for they shall
obtain mercy" (Matthew 5:7).

This is the principle which on its negative
side is the practice of never despising or
judging others, and positively is the active
principle of compassionate understanding
of need in others, and wisdom in knowing
how to meet that need. The Lord touched
upon this principle in 7:1-5—"Judge not,
that ye be not judged ... and why beholdest

thou the mote that is in thy brother's eye, but considerest not the beam that is in thine own eye?"

The Greek word translated "mercy" is a word meaning "merciful and pitiful compassion." This fifth heavenly principle is concerned with sympathy and understanding of the needs, sufferings, and testings of others besides ourselves—the opposite of which is indifference to others and contempt of their weaknesses. There are many sayings of the Lord which seem to indicate that contempt of others is one of the most deadly of all spiritual poisons.

If there is one heavenly principle more than another which the average Christian of this present generation seems likely to forget and neglect, it is this one, for how we do indulge in the unheavenly practice of criticizing and judging others, of talking spitefully or slightingly about them; a habit which simply murders the lovely qualities of mercy, gentleness, compassion, and understanding, which the Holy Spirit so longs to cultivate in our hearts.

Every day our Lord met and dealt with multitudes of blemished, difficult, and defiled human beings. It was not just their crippled, unclean, diseased bodies which needed his healing touch, for our bodies are so often a mirror reflecting the diseases and needs of the inner man, that is, of our souls. When he saw these multitudes, Matthew tells us that "he was moved with compassion on them" (Matthew 9:36). And he helped them.

To him, all the hideous expressions of sin in the lives of men and women appear as so many symptoms of a terrible inner disease, and as such they call forth from him, not angry condemnation and wrath, but passionate concern, infinite compassion, and inexorable determination to save such ruined creatures.

He wants this same attitude of mercy and compassion to be evident in his followers as they serve him by helping the debased, wicked, stupid, and cruel. Yet is it not true, more often than not, that symptoms of sin and degradation in others awaken in us exactly the opposite feelings and attitude of heart. We forget that it is written, "God sent not his Son into the world to condemn the world; but that the world through him might be saved" (John 3:17). We forget that condemnation and contempt wither and blight and kill, whereas mercy and compassion can save and cast out the unclean powers which have brought such lives into bondage and degradation. Over and over again the Lord emphasized divine mercy: "Go ye and learn what that meaneth, I will have mercy, and not sacrifice" (Matthew 9:13); and "If ye had known what this meaneth, I will have mercy, and not sacrifice, ye would not have condemned the guiltless" (Matthew 12:7).

Possibly not a few who are reading this

will know what it is to have friends or acquaintances who are simply tormented by debasing habits and other enslaving things from which they cannot break free: unclean thought habits, unclean bodily vices, harmful drugs, alcoholism, almost insane temper, so they lose control of themselves completely. Are we allowing Christ to help them through us?

It cannot be too strongly emphasized that unless we allow the Holy Spirit to "cut off" from us completely habits of criticism, gossip about others, tittle-tattle, and all judging, despising, and condemning thoughts about others, we cannot expect God to use us.

It is possible that though some of us are known to be Christians, people do not come to us seeking help in their need, and are quite unwilling to accept the helpful advice which we would thrust upon them. They remain completely uninterested in the exhortations which we offer concerning their need to receive Christ into their lives. Perhaps they sense in us judgment and condemnation and the desire to force them to change. It is very noticeable in the Gospel accounts that the Lord never forced his help on others or spoke to them about their need until he had already won their confidence through his compassion and obvious understanding. They went to him for help because his mercy was obvious to all. They will come to us, too, of their own accord when we allow our Lord to develop in us this fifth be-attitude.

GENTLENESS

"Thy gentleness hath made me great,"
    And I would gentle be;
'Tis Love who plans my lot, not fate;
    Lord, teach this grace to me,
When gales and storms thy love doth send,
That I with joy may meekly bend.

Thy servants must not strive nor fight,
    But as their Master be;
'Tis mercy wins, not force nor might,
    Lord, teach this grace to me.
Though others should resist my love,
Keep me as gentle as a dove.

Compassion has such mighty power
    To cleanse and to set free;
Thy mercies save us hour by hour,
    Lord, teach this grace to me.
Thy gentleness hath made me great,
Through me, Lord, others liberate.

The Pure

"Blessed are the pure in heart: for they shall see God" (Matthew 5:8).

The meaning of the word "pure" is "clean, unsoiled, innocent, sincere, unfeigned," or, as we say, "clear as crystal." It is the principle of absolute truth and honesty, and the Lord enlarges upon it in 6:1-18, where he gives one of the most vivid descriptions of the nature of hypocrisy to be found in the Bible.

To be "pure in heart" means to be absolutely sincere. That is to say, all our words and actions must be in perfect harmony with the secret, inner will of the heart; never to say one thing and mean something else; never to attempt to appear outwardly quite different from what we are inwardly. The actions and words of the man who is "pure in heart" are a crystal-clear reflection of the motives and intents of his heart; whereas in the case of a hypocrite, his words and actions are a distorting mirror, seeking to display that which is not true. Thus purity of heart (will) and hypocrisy are direct opposites. The hypocrite desires above everything else to veil the true thoughts and purposes of his heart, because he knows they would awaken disapproval and condemnation from others and, if openly expressed, would bring punishment as well. If he can get away with fulfilling these desires and purposes in secret, and so keep his good name and still appear well in the eyes of men, he is perfectly satisfied. He sets his own standard and sees as good only that which benefits himself and gratifies his own desires.

The "pure in heart" are blessed because "they see God." Now God is the source and origin and sum of all goodness, and only those who practice this heavenly principle of sincerity and truthfulness in all things can see and know what goodness is. They alone can know the true God. For every falsity in our lives must result in a distorted conception of God.

In the passage in Matthew 6, the Lord drew attention to three examples of flagrant hypocrisy and dishonesty to which religious people are liable.

First, he denounced hypocrisy in almsgiving, or as we today would express it, "giving to the Lord's work," or "church and missionary donation," or "gifts to philanthropic and humanitarian causes." If this does not come from the pure motive of using the Lord's money as he directs, but from motives of desiring "praise in the eyes of men," or to put it bluntly, "showing off" and attracting attention to our own generosity and devotion to the Lord, we sin! Not of course that any of us would "blow our own trumpet" in this matter (any more than the Pharisees did) but we do make sure that others make our gifts known while we modestly remain silent ourselves; we are deeply offended and angry if such gifts are not openly acknowledged.

As we have already seen, in another place our Lord referred to what in his day was called "Corban," or gifts paid into the Temple treasury. Many such gifts, he insisted, were given merely to win applause from men, and the money ought really to have been used for the more mundane and unglamorous purpose of supporting aged parents or even difficult and perhaps grumbling and ungrateful relatives depen-

113

dent upon such help. All such gifts given to "the Lord's work" instead, and with the motive of earning applause and a name for generosity or a position of influence and power, the Lord described as hypocritical giving, and as not being given to God at all but merely to buy a reputation on earth.

Secondly, he drew attention to another form of hypocrisy, this time in connection with fasting, which, in its broadest sense, can be taken to mean any kind of self-denial and abstaining from food, pleasure, or comfort of any sort in order to be able to help forward the Lord's work.

Even this can be done ostentatiously; either by the flamboyant advertisement practiced by the Pharisees, or simply by taking care that the "right people" hear about it and will tell others. In a word, the spirit which hates to do good in secret, but must have an admiring and appreciative audience, is not pure.

Thirdly, the Lord spoke of hypocrisy in prayer. Many of the Pharisees were very fluent pray-ers in public, and some of the rabbis were undoubtedly quite fluent preachers—and so are many Christians! But if the words which we use in our petitions are not an expression of real desires in our hearts, but merely an expression of pious ideas which will sound fine to the ears of others, then, said the Lord, it is hypocritical praying. "For the Lord looketh upon the heart," and the real desires which he sees in our hearts are the prayers of which he is conscious. How different the real desires may be from the words we utter! For example, we know that he has said that we should pray for our enemies and for those who have despitefully used us, and perhaps we have dutifully prayed aloud that God will bless our enemies, or those malicious and spiteful neighbors who make life so difficult, while all the time our secret desire is that they may soon be humiliated and suffer as we would like to see them suffer!

The principle of utter truthfulness, sincerity, and honesty is, of course, not only to be practiced in connection with spiritual things, but just as earnestly in secular matters also. This heavenly principle absolutely forbids "wangling" to get our own way by hook or by crook, or justifying crooked dealings done in secret because "everybody else does the same," or trying to get away with some dubious transaction without being found out. For no heavenly power can possibly be transmitted along a line which has been cut at any point by dishonesty and untruthfulness.

The power of leadership and of being able to lead others to see God's will and purpose, to influence others for good, yes, to influence and lead men and whole nations throughout the world, depends on our practicing this principle of "purity of heart," crystal-clear truth. True leaders are not those who use force and compulsion.

Far from it. The real leaders are those who practice absolute sincerity, integrity, and passionate loyalty to truth at any cost, who will even lay down their lives for the truth. These are the men and women who in the end become leaders in the world and are followed even by succeeding generations. For they "see God" and press toward him, and multitudes follow where they lead.

GOODNESS

Goodness is such a lovely thing,
  'Tis Love's own bridal dress;
The "wedding garment" from our King
  Is spotless righteousness.
And those who keep "the Royal law"
Shine lily-white without a flaw.

O blessed holy ones! each day
  Their cup, filled to the brim,
Love's table spread for them, they may
  As God's guests, feast with him.
Their happy faces shine with bliss,
Their joy from him, and one with his.

Goodness is perfect harmony,
  The flawless form of grace!
The golden mirror, where we see
  Reflections of God's face.
Goodness is wrong changed, and put right—
'Tis darkness swallowed up in light.

The Peacemakers

"Blessed are the peacemakers: for they shall be called the children [sons] of God" (Matthew 5:9).

The word "peacemaker" means "to restore harmony, unity, and concord." This heavenly principle the Lord enlarged upon in 5:21-26, where he emphasized and warned against the inner reactions of the heart which lead to disharmony and breaking of the union which should exist between members of the human race. Quite simply, the root causes of all discord, separation, division, and disunity are: anger at one another, indifference to the feelings of one another, and contempt of others (v. 22). Jesus summed up the practical implications of this seventh heavenly principle concerning the peacemakers or restorers of harmony when he said, "If thou rememberest that thy brother have aught against thee ... first be reconciled to thy brother, and then come and offer thy gift" to God (Matthew 5:23, 24).

Broken, sin-diseased relationships within mankind and in the body of Christ can only be healed through the power of God working through his "peacemakers," that is to say, through individual men and women (and groups of them) who have already been brought back into contact with the life and healing power of the head of the Body, the Lord Jesus Christ, and who are thus able to share his life with those who are still separated from it.

Today many doctors have become convinced, just as saints in earlier generations were, that a great deal of physical disease has a spiritual cause, and is the result of continuous breaking of heavenly principles. When such patients are helped to realize this truth and to turn from all poisonous thought habits and reactions and all wrong attitudes of heart, and to begin obeying God in daily life, their physical diseases can often be healed in the most wonderful way.

For instance, it is now known that many bodily diseases can result from habitual jealousy and envy, covetousness, self-pity, restless straining to attain a certain position in the world, stubborn self-will and determination to get one's own way, a passion to alter other people and make them what we think they ought to be, refusal to forgive, constant brooding on wrongs, refusal to face up to the demands which life makes upon us, the habitual effort to evade what we fear and dread, and anxieties of all kinds.

All these inner disharmonies and poisonous attitudes of thought can play havoc with the body, poisoning it, upsetting nerves, glands, digestive system, and every other bodily system and function.

Any kind of healing which does not deal with the spiritual causes of physical disease, if spiritual causes are present, or does not bring them to the consciousness of the patient, nor challenge and empower him to go free from such things, cannot work a permanent cure. The reason for this is it deals with symptoms only and does not touch the root cause of the trouble. "Suggestive" patients, who quickly respond to psychic healing and magnetic personalities, often succumb to some other physical disarrangement and illness, solely because the spiritual cause of their disease has not been dealt with. We remember that all the Lord's healing miracles were done in conjunction with his preaching and teaching of the laws of the Kingdom of heaven, and when he authorized his disciples to heal also, he first commissioned them to preach and teach the same things and put physical healing as a secondary consideration, for it was to follow response to the teaching. It is true that he healed everybody who sought his help, but always he challenged them to have faith in him, that is to say, to respond to him in obedience and to practice the things which he taught.

Peacemaking, of course, involves much more than physical healing. It can also have to do with ministries of reconciliation as Jesus' modern-day disciples bring peace to those alienated from one another, or show others the way out of their prisons of prejudice (racial or otherwise), hatred, distrust, and fear.

Because we have found peace with God and with ourselves through the Prince of Peace, we can now promote peace in others' lives, but only as we faithfully follow our Lord.

PEACE

In acceptance lieth peace.
  O my heart be still!
Let thy restless worries cease
  And accept his will.
Though this test be not thy choice,
It is his—therefore rejoice!

In his plan there cannot be
  Aught to make thee sad.
If this is his will for thee,
  Take it and be glad!
Make from it some lovely thing
To the glory of thy King.

Cease from sighs and murmuring,
  Sing his loving grace.
This thing means thy furthering
  To a "wealthy place."
From thy fears take his release,
In acceptance lieth peace.

The Persecuted

"Blessed are they which are persecuted for righteousness' sake: for theirs is the kingdom of heaven" (Matthew 5:10).

This principle is enlarged upon in 5:43-48, where the Lord challenged his disciples, saying, "Love your enemies, bless them that curse you ... pray for them which despitefully use you, and persecute you" (v. 44).

It is interesting to notice that this eighth principle carries with it the same promise as the first one—"theirs is the kingdom of heaven." The first Beatitude which calls upon us to consider nothing our own, humbling ourselves before God, shows us the way into the Kingdom of heaven and gives us the right to become citizens in it. This eighth Beatitude sets the seal upon all the others, asking us to do the seemingly impossible—love those who hate us.

This is the heavenly principle of forgiveness, which of course can only be practiced in actual fact when we experience wrong done to us by others, or suffer in any degree from the hatred and malice of others, or their despiteful treatment, or actual persecution at their hands. Our Lord experienced bitter persecution and malice and hatred; he accepted it in such a way that it is described by a special word—for it was said of him, "Who his own self *bare* our sins in his own body on the tree" (1 Peter 2:24).

The real meaning of forgiveness is this willingness to bear the wrong done against us by others and all the consequences of that wrong, instead of the wrongdoer himself bearing them or being punished for them. Substitution is an essential element of forgiveness. If someone steals twenty dollars from your wallet or purse, can you accept that loss without holding a grudge or demanding retribution? If not, you have not forgiven the thief.

There are men and women practicing this heavenly principle of forgiveness in our day and generation in a wonderful way. One example which has made a tremendous impression upon my own mind and heart is the testimony of a bishop who was being cruelly tortured at the hands of Chinese Communists, and once, when the pain forced a cry of agony from his lips, his torturers sniggered. He tells us that, undergoing torture as he was, and apparently helpless in the hands of those cruel men, there welled up in his heart such compassion and pity for them that it swallowed up everything else. He felt God's own heartbroken pity for men so devilishly debased that they could find hideous pleasure and amusement in such cruelty.

There was infinite compassion in the heart of the Son of Man as he hung upon the cross, for the men who had been made so callous and hard by their frightful "duty" that they could indifferently nail living human bodies to gibbets. There was compassion and forgiveness in his heart also for the still more devilishly disfigured human souls in the bodies of those religious leaders who stood by the cross mocking him and "wagging their heads in derision" while he suffered.

This book contains only lessons in the Primary Class concerning these heavenly principles. But the far, far smaller persecutions and sneers and unkindnesses and despiteful behavior and willful misunderstandings which come our way provide the training ground on which to begin practicing forgiveness.

As I have traveled and talked with many,

many people, and listened to their stories and the situations which they have described, the thing which has struck me most of all has been the realization of the almost heart-breaking opportunities to practice forgiveness which so many of God's people have! Even in homes which are called Christian, what secret unfaithfulness there may be, or even open desertion. Love grown cold, tyrannical selfishness, habitual thoughtlessness, dishonesty, cruelly wounding attitudes and words. No, these things are not really uncommon, and much else besides, even in the homes of churchgoers in "Christian" lands. But when we remember the sufferings and persecutions endured by multitudes in non-Christian lands, the numbers who must suffer the loss of all things, including their dear ones, in lands where there is terrorism or Communist oppression, then we realize just why this saying of our Lord, "Love your enemies ... pray for them which despitefully use you and persecute you," seems too hard a saying to accept. Yes, forgiveness is the highest of the heavenly laws and the one we are slowest to practice.

Everything which we experience in our own lives, too trivial in comparison with real persecution, but such things as willful selfishness and thoughtless unkindness, these are the experiences in which we who are still in the Primary Class may begin to practice this principle. We must first learn to overcome these smaller evils. Those with whom we live and work provide, perhaps daily, just the opportunities which we need in order to become experts in forgiveness.

LONG-SUFFERING

Love will bear and will forgive,
   Love will suffer long;
Die to self, that she may live,
   Triumph over wrong.
Nothing can true love destroy,
She will suffer all with joy.

From resentment, love will turn,
   When men hate, will bless;
She the Lamb-like grace will learn,
   To love more—not less.
Only bearing can beget
Power to pardon and forget.

Love must give and give and give,
   Love must die, or share!
Only so can true love live
   Fruitful everywhere.
Love will bear the cross of pain,
And will conquer death and reign!

The Slandered

The Lord explained all this further in saying, "Blessed are ye, when men shall revile you, and persecute you, and shall say all manner of evil against you falsely, for my sake. Rejoice, and be exceeding glad: for great is your reward in heaven; for so persecuted they the prophets which were before you" (Matthew 5:11, 12).

In the eighth Beatitude the word for "persecute" is not so strong as that used in this ninth Beatitude. Here the Lord speaks of persecution in a yet intenser form, as though it is "put in rapid motion," "pursued with malignity," and carried to the further and most ardent extremes. In this ninth Beatitude, however, the emphasis is not so much upon physical persecution as moral persecution; the imputation of evil where only good is present, the distortion of truth into falsehood, of purity into impurity; in a word, slander and defamation of character and lying accusation. It refers to punishment meted out to the innocent as though they were really guilty of the most vile of crimes.

It is one thing to suffer as an acknowledged martyr for the truth, quite another to be made to appear as an evildoer suffering only what is just and right! Our Lord described this kind of persecution in the words, "When men shall revile you and ... say all manner of evil against you falsely...." That is where the sharpest and most bitter sting of all must lie!

He briefly enlarges on this ninth heavenly principle in 5:33-37, but we are apt to miss the point of his teaching on this subject: "Ye have heard that it hath been said ... Thou shalt not forswear thyself, but shalt perform unto the Lord thine oaths" (v. 33).

The meaning of the word "forswear" is to break a promise given on oath. The Lord, however, goes on to say: "But I say unto you, Swear not at all," perhaps not even in giving evidence concerning one's own innocence when falsely accused in a law court. James, the Lord's own half-brother, refers to this point in a very emphatic manner in his epistle and quotes the Lord's words: "Take my brethren the prophets ... for an example of suffering affliction, and of patience... Ye have heard of the patience of Job" (whose friends falsely accused him of secret wickedness). "Above all things, my brethren, swear not ... but let your yea be yea; and your nay, nay; lest ye fall into condemnation" (James 5:10-12).

In his own personal experience, the Lord knew more of this form of persecution than anyone else. Over and over again the religious leaders accused him of working miracles by the power of Beelzebub and of being possessed by the devil. All the good he did was ascribed to satanic forces of evil. When he hung upon the cross, he was put there as a malefactor suffering just punishment for the two crimes which at that time were considered most meriting of death. By his own nation he was accused of the most audacious wickedness known to a Jew, that of blasphemy. The accusation against him was, "Making himself out to be God."

On the other hand, Pilate, the Roman governor, could not crucify him on that charge, because it was a religious one and outside his jurisdiction. By Roman law no one could be put to death on a charge of blasphemy against a God in whom the Romans did not believe. So a second false charge was made, a political one. He was accused of sedition, of plotting against Caesar, claiming that he was the rightful King of the Jews and was therefore a rival of the great Roman Emperor who had conquered the Jews.

Pilate was well aware that this was a false charge, made by witnesses paid to perjure themselves. Even under such circumstances, the Lord refused to swear to his own innocence.

On the strength of these two lying accusations of blasphemy and political intrigue, of which he was absolutely innocent, the Lord went to the most brutal and most agonizing death that men had ever invented—a death reserved for only the most wicked of malefactors. He, the spotless Lamb of God, was publicly declared to be worthy of that death because he was convicted of these two crimes.

There is not a single word in the Gospel accounts, nor in the Epistles, to show that the Lord ever referred to either of these charges made against him, or sought to vindicate himself. He remained silent before his judges. He knew that they knew he was innocent. He offered no evidence at all to prove his innocence when those lying charges were made. It was persecution by wicked men, and he submitted to it. All the evidence was so obviously false that in the end Pilate took water and washed his hands in front of Jewish leaders, saying, "I am innocent of the blood of this just person" (Matthew 27:24).

It is under such circumstances (though of course to a far lesser degree) that this ninth heavenly principle is to be practiced. It is not wrong to state our innocence, but when men continue wrongfully and falsely to accuse us, then we are not to insist on self-vindication and self-justification, but to willingly suffer as Christ and the prophets did, and leave God to vindicate us in his own time.

Now undoubtedly this is the hardest and most challenging of all the heavenly principles. It is one thing for a Christian to suffer a martyr's death, publicly accused of what is true; a witness to his faith in things which other men disbelieve; for then all men know that he is bearing witness to his faith, and honest people can at least admire and understand that he is courageously suffering for his convictions.

But it is quite another thing for a man to be sentenced either to death, or to have all his possessions confiscated, on a completely false charge and to be called upon to suffer for things of which he is perfectly innocent, and to be made to appear in the eyes of men as suffering only what is his rightful due, guilty of wicked crimes which he had never committed.

In actual fact slander, the making of the righteous to appear as evil, is far harder to bear than any suffering for the truth. One of the two thieves crucified with the Lord fully realized this when he exclaimed, "We indeed ... receive the due reward of our deeds: but this man hath done nothing amiss" (Luke 23:41).

Undoubtedly this was the thing which the Son of God found hardest of all to bear. And all loving and holy souls must always find it so too. The lust for self-vindication is very strong in all of us. By God's grace some have been able to say, "Yes, I am willing to suffer and, if need be, die for the truth, but let men know the true reason why I thus suffer. They must not suppose that I am really guilty of evils which I have never committed. Why, that would mean that I die in vain! To make out that I myself am guilty of the very things which I most abhor and against which I have publicly preached and protested—no—that is intolerable! God certainly must not allow that."

But our Lord Jesus Christ accepted even that—yes, and forgave it.

This is forgiveness on the highest and greatest scale possible. It is bearing carried to the furthest possible limit. In a real sense, it means appearing before others as actually embodying the evil which we most hate. "He hath made him to be sin for us, who knew no sin" (2 Corinthians 5:21).

It is the Highest descending to the lowest

depths of all. "He humbled himself ... unto death, even the death of the cross" (Philippians 2:8).

Forgiveness practiced on this highest level of all allows God to work in his children with all the power of Pentecost. It is the way to be baptized in fullest measure with the Holy Spirit of love and thus be able to win others to our Savior, Jesus Christ.

The world waits for another Pentecost when the Holy Spirit can work unhindered in men and women. But he can only so come upon us when we, like the first Christians, see what they saw—that these heavenly principles taught and practiced by Christ must be accepted as the standard for ourselves also.

LOVE

Love has made a marriage feast,
    Called each wedding guest,
Rich and poor, greatest and least,
    All at Love's behest
Gathered here to celebrate
The harvest of his joy so great.

See the King's Son with his bride!
    Wooed, and now possessed;
Here behold her at his side,
    In his glory dressed.
This is what he chose her for,
To be his forevermore.

Love has triumphed, Love has won!
    Fruit from sorrow this!

All he purposed he has done,
    She is wholly his.
All her heart and all her soul
Yielded to his full control.

To sum it all up—the New Testament clearly reveals that Christ's followers are challenged to live a Christlike life, as the recipients of supernatural powers greater than any known to ordinary people even in this atomic age—the power of God. "But ye shall receive power, after that the Holy Ghost is come upon you: and ye shall be witnesses unto me..." (Acts 1:8). "That I may know him, and the power of his resurrection..." (Philippians 3:10).

May the Lord who came to earth to teach us these heavenly laws enable us to yield to him with a new understanding of what he longs to bring about in our own individual lives. May he empower us to begin practicing these primary lessons "till we all come in the unity of the faith, and of the knowledge of the Son of God, unto a perfect man unto the measure of the stature of the fulness of Christ" (Ephesians 4:13), who when he taught these things to his disciples summed them all up in a tenth Beatitude—"If ye know these things, happy [blessed] are ye if ye do them" (John 13:17).

CHAPTER 6
Supernatural Living

No one who reads the New Testament with an honest and open mind can fail to be startled, perhaps even staggered, by the description it gives of the kind of life lived by the apostles and the early Christians, and the powers which they possessed and used, a life to which we are obliged to give the name "supernatural."

Neither can we escape the fact that the quality of life normal to Christians in these days is quite startlingly unlike the original pattern as described to us in the Gospels and in the Acts of the Apostles. It is, all too obviously, lived on quite a different and far lower level. Yet, as we read the New Testament, it is equally clear that all Christians are offered the same kind of life which Christ offered to his first followers, and are challenged, even commanded, to live it. This means that we twentieth-century Christians are meant to experience and enjoy the same "eternal life" and to possess and use the same supernatural or "heavenly powers"—powers belonging to "the world to come," as the writer to the Hebrews describes them (6:5). For the New Testament pattern is the normal standard of life which Christ, the Son of Man, promises to all his followers and means for them to enjoy and use for the forwarding of his own purposes here on earth.

When we study the life of the Lord Jesus himself, and read of the powers which he possessed, we only fail to be startled by them (and equally startled as we compare them with our own unhappy earthliness and powerlessness) because we tell ourselves that he, as the Son of God, had unique powers which of course other men are not meant to possess. For years it never entered my head that those very same heavenly powers are the standard and norm for all his followers, and that not only did his first disciples also live lives of tremendous power, but that he actually said to them, "He that believeth on me, the works that I do shall he do also; and the greater works than these shall he do; because I go unto my Father" (John 14:12).

Nowhere in the New Testament is there the slightest hint that this promise was only meant for the apostles, for it says, "He that believeth on me"; and moreover, he "called other seventy also" and gave them the same power! Nor is there a single verse to suggest that this promise was only meant for the first generation of Christians until the "faith" was established and there would be no more need for Christians to live a supernatural or heavenly life on earth, or to possess supernatural powers unknown to ordinary men and women not yet changed into new creatures by a new birth of the Spirit.

In this generation, most of us who are Christians have come to take it for granted that, for some reason or other, far back at a very early stage in the Church's history, there was no longer need for Christ's followers to possess the powers which he possessed; though of course we would not dare to say there was no need for them to live the kind of life he challenged his disciples to live. Most unhappily, however, we find ourselves completely unable to live on the level of victory and fruitfulness and influence on which they lived.

We fail to see the truth. The disciples and the early Christians possessed those remarkable powers simply and solely because they obeyed the Lord's challenge, entered into the Kingdom of heaven, and lived obeying and practicing heavenly principles. As children of God and thus citizens of the Kingdom, they experienced the power of God in their lives—not because they obeyed some magical heavenly formula, but because they obeyed their Lord and so grew spiritually strong and usable by the Master.

The Lord himself did not possess great spiritual powers while he lived on earth simply because he was the Son of God, for when he appeared on earth as Son of Man, he "laid aside" his glory and "emptied himself," taking on our human nature and limiting himself to what is possible to men who know God. (See Philippians 2:5-8.)

So many of us have never even dimly suspected the vital significance of this point. He declared that he came into the world to do two things. First, to show us the Father. Second, to show us how we may become sons and daughters of God and share the life of the Father, by entering into the Kingdom of heaven and living a godly life, in harmony with the heavenly laws, even while here on earth. The Lord Jesus Christ, the Son of Man, did nothing which is not possible and indeed normal for all men and women to do after they receive the life of God. He was the pattern and standard of what God purposes for all men, and the standard he looks for and expects in all

Christians as they gradually mature in the heavenly life during their time here on earth.

What a revolution occurred in my own thoughts and life when I realized this absolutely vital fact!

To live according to the heavenly principles, consistently and continuously, does turn natural men and women into supernatural men and women, possessing and able to use what ordinary men and women would have to call "supernatural power." The gospel of Jesus Christ calls every one of us to this experience—to enter into and live in the Kingdom of Heaven.

The Scripture tells us how to remain in contact with God, so that we will grow and develop, with no symptoms of retarded development. Jesus summed it all up in the words, "Abide in me, and I in you"; namely, remain abiding or plugged into the power of God and his perfect pattern for your life. This abiding refers to abiding in his will, putting our wills down into his, moment by moment and day by day, and finding that we love to do it and that not a single good lies outside the center of God's will. In his will lies our heaven, and every good and perfect thing is to be found there and there alone. Nothing outside his will for us can ever satisfy us, no matter how delightful and desirable it may appear to be.

However, we shall find that we cannot "abide," plugged into God's will, unless we obey God consistently and so practice the presence of God.

All this began to break upon me with a dreadful shock! I discovered that I had not sufficiently developed the spiritual life which follows the new birth, and therefore knew practically nothing about the glorious realities enjoyed by earlier Christians. Indeed, I had tacitly relegated powerful spiritual living to the "abnormal" experiences of the mystics, and supposed that only people who went into trances and ecstasies and saw visions and heard voices and such things ever claimed to be in touch with the spiritual world. I now began to discover that this is not the truth. Certainly most of the mystics and prophets of old experienced these things, but they are not what is referred to here. Countless multitudes of humble and devout Christians who never went into a trance, nor experienced an ecstasy, nor saw a vision, have most certainly had conversation in heaven and have based their life on spiritual reality. They knew God—he was their life. They have, quite literally, lived in the "heavenly places."

A wonderful and transforming joy comes from serving God instead of ourselves. Jesus said it was like being "born again" because this completely new experience of contact with God, of living in him and drawing his life into us with every breath, awakens life in us, and will grow and develop in us day by day (if we nourish it in the way

Jesus teaches us). "This is life eternal," said Jesus, "that they might know thee the only true God, and Jesus Christ, whom thou hast sent" (John 17:3).

We all know what emphasis the Lord laid upon the importance of faith, because it is the first spiritual sense by which we make contact with the eternal world all around our prison house of the physical senses.

In the Hebrew language hearing and obeying are expressed by the same word. Every Hebrew-speaking mother says to her child, "Hear me!" when she wants to say, "Now do what I tell you." That is why it is so important for us to remember that in the Bible sense of the word, faith includes obedient response. If we do not respond obediently to the Savior, we are not exercising true faith. To believe things about him only has to do with the intellect, but to respond in obedience is faith, exercised not simply in the mind, but in the very heart or will.

These days belief and faith are so often supposed to mean mere acceptance of the Christian doctrines and teaching, and acknowledging them as true and much better than the teaching and doctrines of any other religion. That of course is the beginning of faith; for who is going to step out and commit himself completely to One in whom he has no real confidence and whose teaching he does not really believe? But intellectual confidence is shown to be living faith which puts us in vital contact with all the power of God when we begin to respond in fullest obedience to our Lord and Savior.

The Lord himself said, "My sheep hear my voice"; and if we know that we hear his voice and seek to obey it, this is the first positive proof that we have really been born again. Yet how many professing Christians admit sorrowfully that they have the greatest possible difficulty in getting guidance because they cannot distinguish if the ideas that come to them are God's voice or their own thoughts.

Our heavenly Father will certainly not treat us less lovingly and understandingly than an earthly parent treats the little toddler who is just beginning to understand the meaning of words and so often does the wrong thing. We may trust him absolutely. It is always safe to try to obey the voice which at first sounds like the voice of conscience, telling us what we ought to do and what we ought not to do now that we have become children of God. Certainly that voice will often urge us to attempt things that we do not want to do, or fear to do because perhaps they look foolish or humiliating or may be misunderstood by others. Indeed, very often in the beginning the "still, small voice" within seems to call upon us to attempt things which we feel completely unable to do. It is like the mother's voice as she urges the crawling infant to stand on its shaky little feet and toddle a step or two. There certainly will be no anger or irritation or blame in her heart when the wobbling little legs give way and her precious darling topples over! We, however, very much dread such a thing happening to us, especially if there are onlookers who will think us crazy or silly. However, nothing but attempting to obey the voice of our Lord will develop the sense of spiritual hearing, just as nothing but attempting to stand will develop the muscles in the infant's legs. As we grow spiritually, we will better hear the Lord's voice.

Willingness to obey is that precious spiritual organ by means of which the spiritual world begins to break in upon our consciousness and to prove its reality by making itself audible to our inner ears. It is then we begin to be certain that the vanished world really is all about us, because the things we hear, when acted upon, prove true. They really work, and they evidence themselves as being real messages coming to us from the true world. Indeed, they work in such a miraculous way that our whole life begins to be modified and transformed because we now live according to advice and directions coming through to us from a world "the natural man" cannot perceive at all. And those messages, as they come through to us, begin to integrate us in a marvelous way into the purposes of God and his whole scheme of things. Gone are all frustration and futility and regrets for an irreparable and lost past. We know ourselves to be actively incorporated into the life of the eternal world. We are walking and talking with the King.

Every obedient child of God knows that this is true and knows it increasingly more easily and certainly, until it becomes the most natural thing in life to be led by that voice which speaks from the world that is absolutely beyond the perceptions of the five physical senses—the glorious, free, beautiful world outside and beyond and around the prison house of the cosmos.

Looking back over my own past life it is, naturally speaking, quite extraordinary the way my earthly life has been directed and influenced and fashioned by what has been heard coming through from the real eternal world, that is, from my Maker and Savior.

There was a time when I simply could not believe in the existence of a God at all, but at last I determined to put it to the test by willingly trying to do his will if he would speak to me. Then a voice which didn't seem to me to be a voice at all, but only my agonized thoughts, told me to yield the dreadful handicap of a stammering mouth and try to witness to him in public. This was the one thing which seemed impossible to do, but when I tried to obey, it worked, for I discovered that obedience put me in contact with spiritual power which until then had been so unreal that I could not believe it existed, save in the wishful thinking of some

Christians. As a result of yielding that stammering mouth, I have had the incredible privilege of traveling around the whole world, speaking and witnessing with a joy and ease which comes through contact with a power completely beyond and outside myself—the power of God.

God does speak to us—through our thoughts and circumstances, but primarily through his Word.

Just think of the things which have been spoken to the great saints and lovers of the Lord in all ages. There have been men and women who so loved that voice and learned through costly obedience to understand it so perfectly that they turned the whole world upside down, brought reformation and revival to whole countries, and changed the beliefs, habits, customs, and actions of mankind. Yet it was all done through obedience to a voice which other men in the prison house of the cosmos would call an hallucination because it came from beyond this world altogether.

Materialists accuse God's people of illusion because they maintain that they have direct contact with another world altogether—an unseen, spiritual world whose existence cannot be proved to men who don't know God. You cannot convince men who have no living spiritual senses by means of which to perceive a spiritual world. It is especially sad if they have refused to put it to the test, and by hardening

143

their hearts against that inner voice have made themselves incapable of discovering whether God is real or not.

It is, of course, also true that many people profess to be guided by God, or by other beings in the spiritual world, who are most certainly deluded, as is proved by the unhappy and disastrous results which follow their supposed supernatural guidance. Spurious claims cannot disprove the reality of the experience of others who are so obviously in contact with the "world to come" (Hebrews 6:5) that the results of that contact bear persistent witness to the truth of what they declare they have heard. There always have been, and still are, multitudes of such true witnesses in all sections of the Christian Church.

The Christian, the one who has come to know God through his Son, should never say no to the will of God when he seeks to reveal it to him, no matter how impossible or costly obedience to him may look. It is beautiful to take the words of Mary, the mother of our dear Lord, as our motto for every moment of our lives; "Whatsoever he saith unto you, do it" (John 2:5).

The Christian life is not primarily a matter of doing, but of being. Being a beautiful example of what the grace and love of God can do in a human life, right through to the end of it, changing it little by little into a lighthouse of love. Being someone who inspires in others a wonderful sense of confidence in God's unchanging love and goodness and faithfulness. Being a continual reassurance to others, not so far on in the journey, that he who has called us to follow our Lord and Master and to grow like him is able to take us to that goal. We can demonstrate right through to the end that God's faithfulness never fails and that he never disappoints our hopes.

I remember, long ago in 1924, when as a morbid, miserable girl of nineteen, handicapped by a humiliating stammer and just struggling out of a nervous breakdown, I went with my father to the Keswick Convention. And there the transforming miracle happened. The love of God, "in the face of Jesus Christ," shone into my lonely, frightened heart, and Charles Wesley's hymn became real in my own experience:—

> Long my imprisoned spirit lay
> Fast bound in chains of deepest night;
> Thine eye diffused a quickening ray,
> I woke, the dungeon flamed with light.
> My chains fell off, my soul went free,
> I rose, went forth and followed Thee.

That day I began a spiritual walk on the shining path along which my Lord and Savior has been leading me ever since (for more than fifty years), a path truly growing brighter with every year that passes.

But did anyone, I wonder, ever start more tremblingly to follow him than I did? I remember looking out on the eager, happy faces of the hundreds of other young people who attended the special evening meetings for youth, many of whom had testified to yielding their lives to God during the convention. I thought fearfully to myself, "I wonder how long they will keep following? How many of them will presently turn back? Will this wonderful new joy in my own heart really last? Will the Lord be able to keep me delivered from those old, dreadful depressions for even one week? Or will it all wash away like a dream?"

Then, as I sat in the big tent, I looked at the faces of some of the "really old" convention speakers on the platform, with their white hair and aging bodies. I noted the joy and peace in their faces and listened to the glad confidence with which they spoke, and I remember how my heart leaped hopefully within me as I thought to myself, "Well, the Lord has certainly kept them for a great many years. He has not failed them during their long journey through this frightening world. They are still radiant and victorious even in old age. Surely he will not fail me either." I remember how comforted I felt as I turned from the eager young faces to the reassuringly happy and strong faces of those older men.

I think that was the first moment that I realized that even old age has a special and beautiful ministry of its own, one which no other age can fulfill so triumphantly, the ministry of being an inspiration and reassurance to the inexperienced younger folk as they start on the untried way. Seen in this light, old age is one of the most responsible and blessed periods in life. Being an example and inspiration and strengthener of the weak, simply by being a demonstration of the grace and love of the Lord who calls us to follow the way that he went—that's a tremendous calling.

I remember asking an expert authority on the subject, a very elderly friend, "Please give me your advice as to the best preparations I can make for enjoying a peaceful, happy, and fruitful old age."

Like most old people, her thoughts moved more slowly than before. She was silent for a few moments and a faraway look came into her eyes, as though she were looking back through the years at the long journey behind her. Then she said, "I don't think one can make any special preparations. Things happen, you know, that you can't foresee. But remember, there is something new every day, if you look for it."

Ah, yes! Every day God sends us new tokens of his loving kindness and tender mercy. How wonderful to be able to reassure ourselves that right through to the end of life here on earth, each day will bring us new blessings and joys if we watch for them. We must look for him to come with just the new grace and support we need. Something brought to us, perhaps by some invisible angel or heavenly messenger, to gladden each day and prevent the feeling of loneliness when bereaved because of lost friends and departed joys. We should watch each day for new, happy things, and disregard the things we would not have chosen, and so rejoice in the sunshine of his love. We are to let "the fruit of the Spirit ... love, joy, peace, long-suffering, gentleness, goodness, faith, meekness, temperance [self-control]" ripen in us to full maturity and mellowness (Galatians 5:22, 23).

I thanked my friend and stored her secret in my heart.

Another element of spiritual growth is this: we must always be absolutely honest both with God and with ourselves. Never, never must we get into the habit of rationalizing or persuading ourselves that something is right or permissible when God tells us that it is not. Never must we allow wishful thinking to take the place of God's will and voice. That is to say, we simply must not persuade ourselves to believe something we know is not true just because we very greatly wish it were, persuading ourselves that it is all right to do something not quite honest or right in order that good may result. Good cannot result from doing what we know is wrong, but only great harm.

It is so easy to tell ourselves that because someone has wronged or deceived us or taken advantage of us in some way, we may do the same to him in return! So easy to persuade ourselves that some word or action was so small and unimportant that we need pay no heed to the niggling uncomfortable feeling deep down in our conscience. But blessed be "niggles"! We should never ignore them, but hurry straight into the light of God's presence and let him show us just what is wrong and why the uncomfortable feeling is there. It may well be that self is trying to deflect us from the highest though most costly good into something less than the best.

Often it can be quite painful to go into the light and face the truth, but how glorious it is to do so, for the truth heals us and sets us free as soon as we obey it, and floods us with heavenly joy. Rationalizing and persuading ourselves that something is all right and permissible, when we know it isn't, leads us further and further into darkness and confused living.

It is God in whom we all live and move and have our being. If we seek him each day and obey him, our individual worlds of experience are transformed. We will experience healing of body, mind, and nerves, and will find that we are gravitating to happy and fortunate things because we are learning to let God "work in you to will and to do his good pleasure." We will slip back into old ways from time to time, but God will lift us up and continue to work in us. We must "press toward the mark for the prize of the high calling of God in Christ Jesus" (Philippians 3:14).

We are to keep looking joyfully and fixedly at the highest ideal that has been revealed to us—Jesus Christ—and to press on toward it with passionate longing and patience. The challenge given by the Lord Jesus to live the beautiful "Kingdom of heaven" life, even here on earth, does often seem to us like a call to fix our gaze on some shining mountain peak far beyond our reach, though it continually beckons us by its splendor and beauty. Then, when at last it may seem that we have actually managed to reach the summit of the high place we looked at so longingly from afar, we discover that there, shining before us, further on and higher up, are other ranges of still higher and more glorious peaks, challenging us to press on toward the highest of all! We never arrive (in this life anyway), but we can never rest content with anything less than the best God has for us.

Paul felt this too. Even at the end of his long life of the most arduous and heroic spiritual mountaineering, he was still gazing adoringly and longingly at yet unreached high places. He exclaimed, "It is not to be thought that I have already achieved all this. I have not yet reached perfection, but I press on, hoping to take hold of that for which Christ once took hold of me. My friend, I do not reckon myself to have got hold of it yet. All I can say is this: forgetting what is behind me, and reaching out for that which lies ahead, I press towards the goal to win the prize which is God's call to the life above, in Christ Jesus" (Philippians 3:12-14, NEB).

Always life offers us lovely new inner adventures and challenges to higher places, involving the laying down, one after another (like a mountain climber making his pack as light as possible), those things which we had not hitherto realized were weights impeding upward progress. What an exciting adventure this life of following the Lamb turns out to be—full of completely new joys and unexpected delights!

"Let us lay aside every weight ... and let us run with patience the race that is set before us, looking unto Jesus the author and finisher of our faith" (Hebrews 12:1, 2).

For many years the greatest problem of my own Christian life was the fact that in spite of all the undoubted blessing and joy which I experienced in my happy service on the mission field, I did not fully enjoy anything like the kind of transformed life which the teaching in the New Testament had led me to expect would be the result of becoming a disciple of the Lord Jesus Christ. I could not possibly suppose that the sort of Christian life I was actually living resembled in the very least the quality of life enjoyed by his first disciples; nor could the witness which I was so earnestly and zealously trying to give to Jews and Moslems, with no results at all discernible, be at all the same kind of radiant and life-transforming witness given by the early Christians.

By becoming a Christian, I myself had certainly begun to be a changed person (and oh, how great that change needed to be!), but I was still so completely earthbound and so constantly under the power of my "besetting sins" that the ascended life in "the heavenly places" of which the Apostle Paul so constantly wrote, assuring his converts that it was the normal experience the ascended Lord intended for all his people, seemed just a lovely dream, but, alas, in reality unobtainable.

As far as I could judge from the writings of the New Testament, such an "ascended life" lifted men and women up to a completely different level of life and put them in touch with spiritual power otherwise unavailable. In the "heavenly places" they lived according to the laws of heaven, practiced those very same laws in their daily life on earth, and, therefore, presumably actually lived in heaven itself.

It was so distressingly obvious that my own life was lived on a completely different level that I was sure there must be more, far more, wrapped up in the phrase "enter the kingdom of heaven" than I had either fathomed or experienced.

At last things came to a crisis in my spiritual life and something extraordinarily like a second conversion took place. We all seem to experience this type of renewal, or recommitment, or whatever you want to call it, if our understanding develops and matures and opens out into new phases of life. Nature suggests such a lovely comparison of this in the trees, which after the death of winter break into a new life of leafage and are altogether transformed; then later on they break out into a new life of beautiful blossom, and last of all, know an even richer phase of life, that of fruit-bearing.

Be that as it may, I myself, with a joy and thankfulness I cannot describe, began to experience a completely new kind of spiritual life. What actually happened was that in my mind a gloriously new understanding began to unfold concerning the truth unveiled to us by the Lord Jesus when he *ascended* into heaven. It also revealed to me what it can mean in the lives of his disciples when they allow him to teach them how to be raised up to an ascended life in the "heavenly places" with him.

Heaven itself began to break into my own consciousness in such a manner as cannot be described in words; yet I do want to try to share what I can, not because I presumptuously suppose that I have seen unveiled the whole truth—for there must be glories upon glories still to see and lay hold of—but because the practical results of such a new understanding are so great. They bring such a release of power, joy, and love as I could not have imagined possible. There must be many other Christians who are longing desperately for such an experience, and therefore it must be right to bear witness to these things.

I discovered my real problem was that I was ignoring the spiritual world, "the things which are not seen" and are eternal. With a shock I discovered that in all honesty I had to confess I was almost a materialist! I was, indeed, a worldly person, because I cared for almost nothing except this world. Yet I so loved the Lord, was so sincerely distressed over my daily lack of victory, and had such a horror of materialism, atheism, irreligion, and "worldly amusements" that I had always hoped and supposed that I was very "spiritually minded." Indeed, secretly, I thought I was much more "spiritual" than the general run of other present-day Christians! Then how could it possibly be true that I was a materialist?

As I pondered on this, my thoughts led me to see more and more clearly that the Scriptures do claim that the "other world" is the real one and ought to be the one most familiar to us. Writing to the Ephesians, the Apostle Paul most emphatically stressed that for Christians an ascended life in the "heavenly places" is the normal experience they are expected to enjoy, and he claimed that it begins here and now, while we still live on earth.

Then why did the eternal world continue to be so unreal to me? And why was this material one so dreadfully real that by comparison it was the real world, while I could only suppose and trust that the other would prove more real after death?

As often as I thought about these things, I concluded with a sigh, "Well, I suppose that as long as I am here in the body, I must 'walk by faith and not by sight,' and the other world is so unreal to me because I cannot see it, nor hear anything from it, nor touch nor feel anything in it. And the reason why everything in this material world is so real to me is because I have such close contact with it, moment by moment, indeed, can never escape from awareness of it."

But I never could evade the conviction that this was not the teaching of the New Testament, which states that the great difference between Christians and men of the world is just this: we are supposed to be natives and citizens of the eternal world and only strangers and pilgrims in this one. We pass through this world as those who look for "a better country, that is, a heavenly: wherefore God is not ashamed to be called their God: for he hath prepared for them a city" (Hebrews 11:16). Indeed, how clear it is that earlier Christians, especially the martyrs, were so much in that other world that nothing which happened to them in this one seemed very important.

New light, new understanding is like a key which unlocks a source of new life and power. That is why I have come to dread above everything else closing the mind to new light, either through obstinate, preconceived ideas, or through fear of falling into error. It seems to me that there is one vital key to development in spiritual understanding and that is—always keep open to new light. For if we sincerely hunger and thirst to know more of the Lord who is the Way, the Truth, and the Life, our heavenly Father will not treat us less lovingly and carefully than does an earthly father. He will not allow us to be deceived. For does not he himself say, "What man is there of you, whom if his son ask bread, will he give him a stone? Or if he ask a fish, will he give him a serpent? ... how much more shall your Father which is in heaven give good things to them that ask him?" (Matthew 7:9-11). Ask God for strength, for understanding, for protection from untruth—he will not refuse you.

Always keep open to new light from God. I think again of the words of an old friend who said, "Remember, there is something new every day. Be on the watch for it." "Dear Lord, please help me to keep looking for all the happy, good things that happen, and to rejoice in them most gratefully and thankfully, and to keep learning and obeying."

Jesus came 2,000 years ago and challenged those in that day and generation to submit to God, and oh, how difficult it was for them to respond to his challenge. And he has continued, in each generation, to demand total loyalty and obedience. Even as Christians, we need to be more responsive to Christ's commands. For there is always more light and truth to break forth through God's Word than we were able to perceive on the earlier levels of our spiritual development. In every generation, however, it has been as difficult, even for godly and religious people, to accept the higher challenge as it was for those God-fearing Jewish men 2,000 years ago.

We have only to read about the experiences of God-sent messengers and reformers whose consciences had been awakened to see a higher standard and ideal of right and wrong than that accepted by the people of their time, to realize what a difficult and costly thing it is to go out and preach everywhere that men should repent of customs and practices which have long been taken for granted and which are sanctioned by their own special religion.

Think of Elizabeth Fry, the Quaker leader, calling upon her nation to repent of its appallingly inhumane prison laws in her day and generation, and the cruel treatment of prisoners. In those days, the father of a hungry family, or even a hungry boy, could be hanged for stealing food. She described the case of a young woman lying in the prison hospital, afraid to love the unwanted babe she was suckling and which she had tried to destroy, because as soon as the babe was weaned the mother was to be taken out and hanged, leaving the child to suffer neglect and lack of love in the poorhouse. Think of the Quakers calling upon Christian people everywhere to repent of war against their fellowmen, and of the evil of using destructive force against other human beings and shedding human blood. Think of the almost unbelievable suffering and persecution which they endured for so long, until at last they were able to bring at least a certain amount of conviction into the understanding of those in authority. Even today we remain almost completely unaware of the condition under which sincere conscientious objectors who refuse to join the fighting forces still suffer in many parts of the world.

Think too of the tremendous opposition and attacks experienced by those who were the first to go forth and preach that men should repent of the custom of keeping human beings as slaves, owning them, buying and selling them in the markets as though they were cattle, with absolute power over them so they could use and dispose of them as they willed.

Today these things fill us with horrified amazement, and it seems impossible that anyone, least of all truly God-loving religious people, could have believed and maintained that these were perfectly permissible practices with strong biblical authority to support them! But our own present horror and loathing of such things is the result of the courageous witness of men and women in earlier generations, who as soon as they perceived a higher standard of goodness than that taught and practiced by the Church in their day, went forth, protesting sin.

Oh, how difficult we too find it in our own day and generation to be willing to be shown the sins of which we have not been conscious or that we are unwilling to deal with, practices which we have taken for granted as being perfectly proper and God-permitted. We seem unable to be willing to lay them aside, no matter how difficult and costly it may be to do so, even involving a change in lifelong habits. Oh, how easy it is for us to claim biblical support for such things as waging wars against enemy aggressors in spite of what Jesus so clearly taught in the Sermon on the Mount. He said we must be willing to love our enemies and to return good for evil and to forgive those who threaten us as aggressors and conquerors, until we can turn them into friends. This is what Jesus taught the people of conquered Israel to do. It is as easy for us today to find biblical justification for such things as racial prejudice, religious discrimination and intolerance, and many other un-Christlike attitudes as it was for Christians in earlier generations to claim biblical support for waging Holy Wars on unbelieving and heathen nations, putting to death those who would not believe in the one true God, and for buying and selling human slaves. Misinterpreted, the Bible seems to sanction such things. And the Bible does give examples of these and other abuses, even when done by the most godly believers (for example, Abraham had slaves). But the Bible does not approve of all that it records.

More than twenty years ago, I once saw a small boy run up to a friend and shout, "I throwed my pill down the drain!" The smile of triumph on his face was a sight to see, but I could not help thinking, "Oh, you foolish little boy! I expect that pill was meant to do you good—why ever did you throw it away? But how exactly like all of us you are, for do we not instinctively try to evade or get rid of the things which we do not like?"

Have we not all discovered that there come periods in our lives when we find ourselves confronted with something very much like a pill which we cannot bring ourselves to swallow, and we are tempted to resist the situation with all our might. I wonder if you have noticed that if we do manage to throw the pill away, there then follows a period when it seems impossible to make any further advance in our spiritual life. Instead, all the earlier joy and power and adventure of following our Lord begin dwindling, bit by bit, and then, like leaves dropping from the trees in autumn, everything sweet and lovely in our lives begins to wither, leaving us with a bitter sense of loss, or of frustration or discontent, or anxiety or loneliness.

It is very striking how many people in these days are passing through an experience of change or loss which to them feels like a bitter pill they cannot bring themselves to swallow. Perhaps it is the departure from home of loved ones or friends, the loss of inspiring Christian fellowship, loss of health, unanswered prayer for healing, a change in the circumstances which made their outward lives happy and blessed, loss of material comforts, or worse still, the apparent ending of happy and fruitful work for God, or some bereavement, which removes from them the central joy of their lives, leaving them with a terrible sense of desolation, of coming to the end of a happy period in life, now to face only a dreary or lonely future.

What a glorious thing it is to realize that such experiences don't have to bring regret or sadness, depending on our reaction to them. Perhaps God is asking us to move on to a greater level of spiritual maturity. God never asks us to let go of anything until he sees that we are ripe and ready to respond to something yet higher and far better than we have been able to experience in the past.

Not only are we forgiven because of Christ's death, but God also asks us to die—to our selfish desires, our own ways of doing things. But death is always followed by resurrection. If we try to resist loss and change or to hold on to blessings and joys belonging to a past which must drop away from us, we postpone all the new blessings awaiting us on a higher level and find ourselves left in a barren, bleak winter of sorrow and loneliness.

Each of us should set apart some time each day for the special purpose of letting God speak to us and show us his will. This, of course, involves reading and studying the life and teaching of our dear Lord Jesus, as expressed in the entire Bible. The best time for this is the first thing in the morning before we do anything else, before our thoughts become engrossed with other things. This is an urgent necessity if we want to continue to grow in awareness of his will. We must learn to feed our minds on his Word and know how to recognize his voice speaking to us and directing us. At first it may be difficult to acquire the habit—to wake earlier, to get up and devote the extra time thus achieved to this purpose. But the results are so wonderful and happy that soon it becomes not a difficult effort, but a joyful and precious special pleasure that we would not miss for the world. I look back over the years and, for me, this habit of an early morning quiet time stands out easily as the most blessed and rewarding aspect of my life. It has been a long vista of shining morning hours in his presence, reading a portion from the Bible, thinking over what I have read, asking him to explain it to me and to show me just how it applies to my own life, and then going out, by his grace, to try and practice what I learned from that reading, and to obey the guidance for the day which he has given.

I am so thankful that I was warned in the very beginning, by experienced friends, that nearly all the people who slip back into indifference admit that it began with neglect of the daily quiet time, and failure to give God an opportunity to speak and to train them to listen to his voice. I myself at first never felt him present, and there was always the inner suggestion, "He isn't real after all. All this is just imagination and wishful thinking." But I learned to take no notice of that feeling and to say, "O God, I know you are real because I experience your help and power. Let me speak to you as I would if I could actually see you. Help me to understand this portion of the Bible which I am reading, and show me what you want me to do afterward as a result of reading it."

Then as I turned to the teaching of Jesus, again and again it seemed as though my thoughts received new illumination and that the passage actually spoke to me. I found that God used my mental faculties, that he spoke to me in my thoughts, and encouraged me to ask questions and to let him direct my thoughts so that the answer came to me through my thoughts too. I found it a great help to write down a little summary of what he said and wanted me to do, in a quiet time notebook, so that I could check up and see if, by the end of the day, I had done what he told me, what the result had been, and whether the guidance had really worked and turned out good and right.

For me there has been nothing passive about all this, no waiting for something to come to me out of the blue. But I find he clarifies my thoughts as I express my questions (often I write them down too), and enables me to think the answers. Often, of course, especially at first, it was my own self's thoughts which came into my mind, but I quickly became able to recognize his answers and the thoughts that were from him, for those thoughts came with a special clarity and sense of rightness. It was as though all of a sudden something would click in my mind. "Oh, that's what he wants me to understand! That's what he wants me to do! So that is the meaning of this Bible passage, or of this puzzling thing that Jesus said! Why did I never see it before?"

For a long time, there was always the suggestion of my senses that he was not real, but a personal interview with him each morning in the quiet time renewed the reality of my relationship with God. As the months passed and he enabled me to obey his leadings, the joy and sense of his reality, and proof after proof that the guidance was right and did work, filled my life with a happiness and assurance I had never before believed possible. As the years pass, of course, it becomes a delight and joy to lengthen the daily quiet time, by rising earlier or foregoing something else, and little by little to continue the communion with him all through the day, until there is no time when he seems unreal or absent from us.

CHAPTER 7
Eyes of Love

Crucifixion is an essential part of the Christian life—not only Christ's crucifixion, but ours. As we die to selfish living, or immoral living, or materialistic living, or fearful living, or arrogant living, or whatever, we move on to higher, more triumphant levels of spiritual experience. Bearing our cross, crucifying our self-centeredness, brings growth in the Kingdom of God.

"Oh," you exclaim, "I couldn't possibly

submit to such a cruel, horrible process as that."

But, you see, if we are willing for it, it turns out to be an unspeakably glorious and happy and wonderful process, for day by day and year by year, we shall find that more and more we begin to gravitate to happy circumstances, and to escape, little by little, from the sad and painful ones. Our whole environment will gradually change and become more and more happy, and our bodies will become full of health and vigor. Whereas if we will not die to the self-centered life, and reject this painful-looking, but really blessed, process of being transformed, God-centered people, we will discover that we ourselves, without knowing it, have been creating a cross on which we must be crucified as the years pass. For as long as we continue to express selfish, self-inspired attitudes and words and actions, we are preparing for ourselves sorrowful and painful experiences. All of us, without the possibility of escape, must have the self life put to death, and we can either voluntarily allow God to do it in his loving, wise, and wonderful way, or we can create experiences which will be so sad and bitter and despair-bringing that in the end, they will seem like a hell from which we cannot escape, and in that condition we shall learn to loathe the very thought of living a self-centered life ever again—we will learn the hard way.

Oh, how blessed it is to follow the example of all the holy men and women in the Bible (and holiness means "devoted, set apart for God's use and service"). Wherever they went they built altars on which they laid down their surrendered wills and offered up to death their own self-will. Who can describe adequately the joy of those who do this and discover as the years pass that every costly act of obedience results in some wonderful and blessed experience, and in new power and closer union with God. Everything voluntarily laid down unto death for his sake is raised again in some more glorious form, and every dying to self and self's will and desires increases the intensity and joy of knowing God. Oh, what fortunate people they are—the most fortunate people in the world, who have learned to say a glad and loving Yes to God. We all forget sometimes, but when we come back to him, his joy is ours again.

One lovely spring evening I went for a walk, meaning to explore a fascinating little wood I had often looked at from afar, and where I hoped I might find some wild primroses. However, when the footpath had actually led me to the wood, I was dismayed to find that every part of the ground beneath the trees was carpeted not with primroses but with stinging nettles. So much so that I beat a hasty retreat. Retracing my steps, I found there was another narrow footpath skirting the whole length of the wood and divided from it by a hedge. It led across a field full of beautiful springing wheat, like a soft sea of green waves, stretching to the horizon—and there was not a single nettle to be seen.

Along this path I walked happily in the golden evening light, all the time only a step or two away from that other path through the stinging wood. As I walked, I meditated on these two different paths, and it seemed to me that they afforded a perfect illustration for the message in this book.

Two paths lie before us in life. The one way is that of devoting ourselves to God, shunning evil, preferring to be faithful servants of the King, even trusting him to use the most difficult circumstances to build us up. When we follow that path, we do indeed many times during each day find ourselves exclaiming, just as I have done ever since this wonderful secret was revealed to me, "Oh, what fortunate people we are! What happy things God causes us to experience when we allow him to control us and to work in us to do his good pleasure."

The other path is the way of self-centered and self-inspired thoughts and words and reactions and behavior. Looking at everything through the eyes of self and seeing only what *we* want, or do not want, and what *we* think about the way in which other people and other nations behave, and pointing out all the faults that we perceive in order to make the faulty persons correct them! My own experience of spending many years of my life acting in that way has given me a very low opinion of its power to produce any good results or alterations. Instead of helping matters, it really is like a path leading further and further into a wood full of briars and stinging nettles. The longer we follow that path, the more we discover that unhappy and unfortunate things are springing up around us, because it is self working in us to express our own selfish will and desires and attitudes. So sorrows and frustrations and sickness of the body or mind, and troubles of all kinds, and disappointments and sorrowful losses become more and more our portion as the years pass.

How encouraging it is to realize that it is possible, by God's grace, to step from the path in the stinging wood onto the path through the field rich in blessings, the moment we are willing to allow God to displace selfishness with an increasing love for him. Almost at once we begin to discover little green shoots of joy springing up around us, and after a few months, and increasingly as the years pass, everything in our lives is made new.

It is true, of course, that we shall continue to meet tests and trials and tribulations, but if we allow God to express his good reactions toward these things, we find that we overcome their power to do us any harm and, miraculously, they are all changed into

171

blessings—what others may enviously call "good fortune." Ah, yes, how fortunate are those who know the Kingdom of God way of reacting to everything that happens, and who obey the Golden Rule: "always treat others as you would like them to treat you" (Matthew 7:12, NEB).

There is a very ancient teaching that if you know the right name of anything, you will have full power to control that thing; but if you call it by a wrong name, you give that thing power over you. Bringing this into a totally Christian perspective, those circumstances, people, or situations we call and see as "bad" will indeed be bad experiences for us. Our reactions to life's problems are the key. If we can see a nuisance as an opportunity to practice heavenly reactions, be certain of this—heavenly results will blossom from it.

During the years when I spent most of my time traveling from country to country, I wanted to have a peaceful, secluded spot in England where I could quietly retreat to my trailer and do my writing work between journeys. I was led to a most delectable spot on the seashore of a little island, and there I happily prepared to enjoy what I called "peaceful seclusion"—only to find very soon afterward that numbers of other people were also discovering what a delectable place it was, until there seemed hardly room to turn around, and even the view of the sea from my windows was completely blocked.

I was sorely tempted to protest such horrible overcrowding. But the loving Inner Voice, the Lord speaking in my thoughts, spoke warningly, "Take care! If you call it 'horrible' you will find it so, and 'crowded out' you will certainly be. Try enjoying and helping your new neighbors, and see what happens."

Amazingly, not all in a moment, but as the weeks and months passed, there they were, simply dozens of them—smiling, friendly, delightful, kind neighbors, sending their children to Sunday school in my trailer, and teaching me all sorts of beautiful and wonderful things about which I had known nothing before.

Of course, I am sometimes tempted to go back to the old way of thinking. But fortunately, having had my attention drawn to this beautiful principle, I can look joyfully for good in every situation as it comes, and what fun it is finding it.

Obviously, this great principle works in comparatively easy circumstances, kindergarten lessons in living. To see its power manifested in fullest glory, one must use it in circumstances which one would be tempted to call "simply unbearable," or "disastrous," or "cruelly unjust," or "utterly wrong" and "shocking." But of course if we give such names as those to anything, we open ourselves to untold woe and misery and, quite possibly, chronic ill health. As the Bible assures us that "all things work together for good to them that love God" (Romans 8:28), quite obviously we ought to maintain a positive outlook, which lets all circumstances work together for good as soon as possible.

The Bible is full of the importance of names, even the names which parents give their children. A good and beautiful name referring to some glorious quality in the nature of God exercised a wonderfully inspiring influence upon the child, and reminded the parents of the holy desire which had been in their hearts when they gave that name. I myself am deeply grateful to my parents for giving me the name Hannah, which means "God's grace," because it reminds me continually of his beautiful promise, "My grace is sufficient for thee: for my strength is made perfect in weakness" (2 Corinthians 12:9).

There is one especially beautiful and inspiring story in Genesis 29:21-35 about a woman named Leah, who sought almost despairingly to remake a situation which we might think she had every reason to call unbearably cruel and miserable. For she found after her wedding that she had been married to a man who believed that she was her younger sister Rachel, whom he adored. He had promised to serve her father without pay for seven years so that he might marry Rachel.

Leah's husband was Jacob, which means "crooked" or "supplanter," and such a name seems to have exercised a most unfortunate influence over him, even from boyhood, as though, subconsciously, he said to himself, "Very well, if you call me supplanter, that's just what I will be!" And for most of his life, we find Jacob struggling with the temptation to deal dishonestly with his relatives and others, deceiving his own blind father and seeking to supplant his elder brother Esau. In the end, but not till twenty years after he had been tricked into marrying Leah, just as he had tricked and deceived others himself, God gave Jacob a beautiful new name, Israel, "prince of God." That new name did indeed work upon Jacob with miraculous power and inspiration, and has become a name in which his descendants glory until this day.

But how terrible for Leah, on the day after her marriage, to discover that it was really Rachel whom Jacob loved. More dreadful still, according to the custom of those times, Jacob, after sullenly promising to serve unpaid for another seven years, was duly allowed to marry Rachel also, just one week after his marriage to Leah. Thus Leah found herself an unwanted wife, with her own younger sister the real and adored mistress of the home.

It is hard to picture any situation more harrowing than that! And when, as time passed, God gave Leah children though Rachel remained childless, we can see from the names which Leah gave to her little sons how bitter she felt.

She named her firstborn son Reuben, which means, "Behold, a son!" for she said, "Surely the Lord hath looked upon my affliction; now therefore my husband will love me" (v. 32).

But though Jacob, in the joy of becoming a father for the first time, may have become kinder to Leah, she was evidently preoccupied with her "affliction" and self-pity, and her situation became worse rather than better. We find her calling her second son Simeon, or "hearing," for she said, "Because the Lord hath heard that I was hated, he hath therefore given me this son also" (v. 33). Dwelling on the bitter fact that she was not only unwanted by Jacob, but actually hated by her jealous sister, made matters still worse. Her third son she named Levi, or "joined," for she said, "Now this time will my husband be joined to me, because I have borne him three sons" (v. 34).

You see, all her hopes and longings, so very naturally, were centered upon gaining her husband's love, and perhaps even triumphantly weaning away his love from his childless wife Rachel. But, all this time, through the sorrows and trials which seemed so unbearable, the loving heavenly Father was helping Leah, and gradually causing something wonderful to happen in her heart, which at last put into her hands the golden key which she so much needed to find and which was to open for her—yes, and for the whole world—a door of marvelous blessing. We know this happened, for when Leah's fourth son was born she gave him a beautifully right name, Judah, which means "praise God," for she said, "Now will I praise the Lord" (v. 35).

At last Leah's attitude was, "No matter if my husband doesn't love me or want me; no matter if Rachel envies me and conspires against me; no matter if I may never experience the fulfillment of my human longing for my husband's love, yet now I will praise the Lord for all his love and goodness in giving me these children. I will be more than satisfied with his kindness, and I will unite my love and my will with his, knowing that even in such a situation as this, all things really will work together for good."

Oh, what wonderful, sacred, and miraculous power there is in trusting God even in dreadful situations! What a glorious thing had happened to Leah! One of the Jewish rabbinical commentators has pointed out that unwanted, brokenhearted Leah is the first person mentioned in the Bible to offer true praise to God, for the word praise is not used in the Bible "until Leah came and praised God." Doesn't that seem to emphasize that real praise is being thankful to God and rejoicing in him even when all our earthly circumstances seem to deny that he is good and loving and wise and faithful. To thank him and trust him when the very worst seems to happen, and to be willing to "wait patiently" for him to unfold his glorious purposes—this is what God looks upon as perfect praise!

But more wonderful still, see what followed Leah's discovery. Not just blessing and comfort for herself, but for her descendants in later generations too—yes, and for the whole world. It was into the tribe of Judah that David was born, the man who became "the sweet singer" and composer of some of the most glorious songs of praise to God which have ever been written. We still sing them around the world today, thousands of years later, in both Jewish and Christian gatherings for worship.

But there is something still more glorious than that! For it was into the tribe of Judah—"praise God"—that, centuries later, Jesus the Savior of the world was born.

Not that we are to swallow resentment and anger, or try to repress our wrong feelings—that is a very unfortunate thing to do. Repressed resentments and dislike and anger can cause very real harm to our bodies and nerves. We are not to swallow our negative feelings and suffer from gastric ulcers and chronic indigestion as a result, but to ask the Holy Spirit of God to change these wrong feelings and thought attitudes. For example, resentment or grumbling can be changed into thanksgiving and gratitude to God for all his goodness to us. We should be thankful that we are fortunate enough to know that if we react with praise and thanksgiving to everything that happens, even to the seemingly unfortunate things, they can bring us blessing and joy. We can praise and thank him for giving us opportunities to practice forgiving others, for this puts us in contact with the highest power of all, God's own forgiving love, which will give us power and help the people we forgive and to awaken in them, gradually or at once, longings to know God too. Anyone toward whom we have occasion to practice continual, perhaps even daily, forgiveness affords us glorious opportunities to develop spiritually. And by forgiving them, we can help them find deliverance from self-centered living. We share in God's own heavenly joy of being able to help other poor people imprisoned in unhappy and dreary worlds of their own making.

The ability to touch and handle things unseen is developed through obedience to the command of the Lord to accept and "take up the cross" and to follow him. This, of course, means to do what he would do, and to react to all the circumstances and tests of life as he himself would react. He always trusted his Father, even while he was on the cross.

We can know quite clearly when we are touching things in the heavenly world by what comes through to our spiritual sense of feeling. And what comes through when we touch eternal things is joy—always joy. It has been said, surely quite truly, that "joy is the hallmark of the Christian." It is the only true standard by which to test our spiritual experience. If joy is largely absent, or dependent upon things going well, we may quite seriously suspect that our spiritual experience, so-called, is a spurious thing.

This seems a dreadfully hard saying, but how thankful I am for God's faithful messengers who have reiterated it for us over and over again. I came to realize at last—with another tremendous shock!—that as long as I was not continuously filled with joy, I was not experiencing the authentic brand of Christian experience promised to us in the Bible.

If joy is continually being extinguished or depends upon things going well and according to my desires, then I certainly am not enjoying the sort of Christian life known to the early Christians, the martyrs, and the true lovers of the Lord in every generation. And this, I have discovered, means that I am not in touch with unseen realities, but taken up with the things of my five physical senses to the exclusion of my spiritual sense of touch and feeling.

Our Lord laid much stress upon this point. He said: "In the world ye shall have tribulation, but be of good cheer" (John 16:33).

Of course this does not mean that we shall never feel sorrow or grief or distress or pain; it means that with the sorrow and grief and all the other natural feelings, there will be unbroken, shining, radiant joy as well—a joy which nothing can take away.

Once again, is this "an hard saying and we cannot receive it"? For how can we be expected to be joyful when our hearts are broken or our loved ones are suffering? Or when we, and they, are being cruelly wronged or exploited by others and everything seems to be against us? Can it be right for us to *feel* joy under such circumstances?

Well, the early Christians and the martyrs managed it. And it is the proof that we really are experiencing the things which the Lord promised to his own disciples and followers when we find that the things which deprive ordinary people of this world of their joy and peace cannot deprive us in the same way. That is because, in the power of the new life of the Spirit of God, we now react to all these things in a completely new way. We are actually able to "count it all joy" when we fall into testings, tribulations, and all kind of temptations. We react with praise and joy comes through.

We are to look upon every situation, without exception, as an opportunity for acting creatively, accepting the thing with praise and with no self-pity or bitterness or resentment, or envy of others. This means reacting with praise and thanksgiving to all the things which wound us, thus putting to death any selfish hopes and desires. It means willing acceptance of everything along the pathway of life, not seeking to evade the difficult or seemingly impossible things—not trying to make out that wrong things are right, but reacting to them in such a way that out of them we bring something beautiful to the praise and glory of God.

It is when we learn to react in this way that we discover we are actually living in heaven, touching heavenly things and feeling heavenly joys. It is through this avenue of acceptance that joy comes through continually.

Therefore, if anyone wants to know what it feels like to live in heaven, this is the way to find out. Let him begin reacting creatively, that is, accepting everything with praise, as an opportunity by which to glorify God, never grumbling, never moaning, never wondering "why has this been allowed to happen?"—and he will soon find that all life's sorrows and testings are thus turned into avenues for feeling the joys of heaven.

And if anyone wants to know what it feels like to live in a self-made hell and to become certain that there is no such thing as a heaven and to feel like the most ill-used and miserable person in the universe, then let him habitually react to life's experiences with resentment, grumbling, self-pity, and angry frustration, and alas! all too soon he will find out. For what comes through to him is darkness and torment, a sense of overwhelming futility, frustration, and despair. It was not without reason that Dante made Despair the capital of hell!

Perhaps, just at this point, someone who is reading this may be thinking, "Well, I can't believe in God, not even that he exists as some kind of power, so this book is not for me. All this talk about the Kingdom of God is just fantasy and wishful thinking, a way of trying to evade the hard realities of life and to escape from facts which will have to be faced sometime, in a world so obviously full of evil.

Well, to tell you the truth, there was a time when I too could not believe in God, and felt just like that myself when people spoke of him. For me it was a time of hopeless despair as I struggled through a nervous breakdown, and woke morning by morning with the dreadful feeling that I could not face another day and all that it would bring me.

But those who have been in that kind of situation, and then, mercifully, have been helped to enter "The Kingdom of God," as Jesus called it, and to find that he *is* absolutely real, that we *can* contact his power and hear him speaking to us and guiding us, can never afterward doubt either his existence or the realm where his will is done. It really is like being "born again," and awakening to life in a new existence altogether. It's like little blind, deaf, and dumb Helen Keller suddenly finding a loving teacher and helper to rescue her from the dark, soundless, terrible pit of loneliness in which she had felt so trapped and lost, revealing to her the way to make contact with a real world which had been there all the time, even though her physical senses of sight and hearing had not been able to perceive it. Jesus is the loving teacher and rescuer who enables us to come to the Father of love and goodness, and to live in his presence and in his kingdom.

How can we awaken to God's glorious realm of light and goodness all around us which we cannot perceive by means of our physical senses, and to which the vast majority of poor human beings are still so blind and deaf that they cannot even believe that it exists.

H. G. Wells once wrote a story about a man who fell over a precipice into a valley isolated from the rest of the world. He discovered that all the people living there were completely blind, and had no eyes in their faces. No one had ever seen the sky and they didn't know what sunlight was like. They were incredibly inventive and clever with their hands, but they believed only in what they could taste and touch and feel. They told him that there was a solid ceiling above their valley, with some mechanical arrangement affixed to it which caused water to fall at certain times and heat to be turned on and off at other times. When he assured them that there was no solid ceiling, but a glorious infinity of sky, filled with stars by night and the glory of the sun by day, and that water fell from cloud galleons sailing in the marvelous ocean of the sky, and that warmth streamed upon them from a glowing heavenly body millions of miles away, they first mocked him for supposing that they were gullible enough to believe such childish fantasies, and then said he was obviously a lunatic and might be dangerous. Finally, they insisted that he must undergo a surgical operation (they had skilled doctors) and let them remove the two soft, twitching, bulging objects which they could feel in his face, by means of which he insisted he could perceive the things he told them about.

Evidently these "eyes" were the cause of his mad delusions. Once they were removed, he would become like them, happily unaware of a dream world of fantastic nonsense, and satisfied with the real, practical world of things which can be eaten and touched. But, rather than lose his precious sight, the man chose to climb again to the foot of the precipice over which he had fallen, and there, in the freezing cold of the mountain night, lie down and die to his fallen life in the Country of the Blind, with his eyes lifted toward the coming sunrise.

Well, if anyone wants to awaken to God and the real world of light, then something like that really must happen, for we must be willing to die to our self-consciousness and self-centeredness and to accept God's rule instead. We must be willing that God should control all our thoughts and desires and words and actions and use every part of us, and all that we possess, for the purpose of expressing his good and glorious will, so that it may truly be said of us, "It is God which worketh in you ... to do his good pleasure" (Philippians 2:13), and "make you perfect in every good work to do his will, working in you that which is well-pleasing in his sight" (Hebrews 13:21).

Oh, what fortunate and happy people we are if we choose the happy and blessed way of voluntary surrender to God's good and glorious will, and enter at once into the Kingdom of God. But we cannot put the self life to death in our own strength. It can only be done when we contact God's power by faith. Quite possibly your heart sinks again at the very word, faith, just as mine used to do, because you know you haven't any faith, and that you simply can't believe, and faith can't be forced. Faith, you say to yourself, means being absolutely sure about something without a single doubt, or like the little boy said, "Making yourself believe what you're sure ain't true!" Wrong!

Faith doesn't necessarily crowd out all doubts right away. But it will certainly grow into that kind of assured certainty later on, simply as a result of experiencing the reality of his presence and of his power to help us.

But in the beginning, as I can testify from personal experience, faith is a tiny seed of willingness to put God to the test, to do what he has told us to do, through the coming and teaching of Jesus, who is the perfect revelation of his will for all of us. I myself could only kneel down and cry in silent despair: "O God, if there is a God anywhere, you must help me. I am willing at last to lay down my own will and to accept yours. If you are really there, make yourself real to me." He awakened in me, then and there, such a wonderful sense of his reality and presence that I have never been able to doubt his existence again! The life which was born in me that day, forty-seven years ago (and I wondered if it would last for even one week!), has remained gloriously present with me ever since, and has grown and developed with each year that has passed.

If you want to join the company of fortunate people who have discovered this wonderful way of life, then all you have to do is to be willing to let God control you completely and to help you to live according to the pattern Jesus showed and taught us, for it is God's will that we should all become exactly like him. Nothing less than that will do, though of course it is a matter of growth, beginning as a tiny baby, and day by day and year by year developing to the "full stature of Christ." The initial step is, of course, spiritual birth.

It is the willingness which is the obedient faith. It is this which puts us in contact with God's power. If we honestly want him, and are willing to obey him, that faith works in just the same way as when you press the plug of your electric kettle into the socket in the wall where it makes contact with the electric current. Faith does just that—it contacts God's power.

Faith is also the willingness to believe what Jesus taught, to respond to his challenge, and to become citizens of the Kingdom of heaven, accepting God's will instead of self-will as the ruling power in our lives.

All this is possible only because of God's love, love which opens our eyes and makes spiritual things real to us. The Kingdom of heaven must remain invisible to those who know nothing of true love.

Although I had been a missionary for twenty years, most happily, I discovered that for all the years of my Christian life I had been like a blind person, led by the hand—directed by the voice of him whom I loved, but wandering in darkness instead of walking in the light of heaven. This was, I now discovered, because I knew practically nothing at all about the "love of Christ shed abroad in my heart" in actual reality. For I had lived all those years in ignorance of how to obey the Lord's one great command, "the royal law of love" as James calls it (2:8). "This is my commandment, That ye love one another, as I have loved you" (John 15:12).

Certainly I had always known well enough in theory that Christians must love one another and should have "a passion for the souls of all men." But how to do so remained a dreadful mystery! There were some people I could not love; some who seemed so annoying and unlovely (I called it un-Christlike, but didn't see how appallingly un-Christlike I myself must be simply because I could not love as he did) that really I did not even want to love them, but only to keep away from them as much as possible.

But God has taught me that no love is real love until it is *willingness to love all,* with no exceptions; and that the more sinful, blemished, and unlovely a person is, the more he needs love. More love—not less—toward those who are obviously spoiled and marred and sin-sick—that's God's way. Then I was shown that love does not begin in the feelings at all—it begins in the will. To be willing at last to love all, individual by individual, as we are brought into contact with them, is to be *able* to love all. We must begin quite deliberately to act toward them as though we really do love them and are willing to bear everything unlovely about them just because we want to love them. Then love comes, first as a trickle, then as a stream, then as a flood, till, like the river of life in Ezekiel, the waters which at first came only to the ankles, then to the knees, then higher still, became at last "waters to swim in."

Love is light, and when love has opened our inner eyes we see things in their true light—a whole new landscape of reality and truth is spread out before us and we see beauties and wonders of the realm of God which we never before even glimpsed, nor suspected to exist. Love is the illuminer of our understanding as far as spiritual matters and truths are concerned, and one cannot help suspecting that the most scholarly and learned theologians and Bible students, if they attempt to unfold the truth, are really like blind men guessing at the appearance of an unknown landscape if they have not first been illumined by love—love to God, and then (and just as necessary) love to one another and even to those with whom they differ in their interpretations of truth.

Personally I have come to feel with great intensity that I dare not trust the teaching of anyone in spiritual things if that one bickers and quarrels with others over doctrinal matters and denounces and condemns fellow Christians, for it must surely mean such an one cannot be a safe guide as far as the Scriptures of Truth are concerned—for those Scriptures are all inspired by the Holy Spirit of love himself. And oh, how I have come to regret the fact that I myself was for so many years such a zealous denouncer of the "unsound opinions" and doctrines of

190

others and allowed myself to despise those who did not see as I, in my blindness, fancied I saw the real truth.

Over and over again the Scriptures tell us that those who love are filled with light and walk in the light and not in darkness. I had read these things over and over again without understanding their real meaning. I had always supposed that love was a delightful feeling felt for some, and most unhappily not felt toward many others! But now I discovered that *love begins in the thoughts* and from there overflows into the feelings. I found, too, that another difference between "heavenly love," *agape,* and "natural love" is that heavenly love does not demand anything likable or admirable in the object to be loved before being willing to love it! For it is not necessarily a love of personalities—at least not at first, nor a liking and natural attraction toward certain persons, but rather it is the desire and will for the happiness and blessedness of all, however undeserving and unattractive they may appear. For sin-spoiled personalities do not awaken liking, but rather compassion and sympathy, and a recognition of complete oneness with them in their and our own need of the love and help of the Savior.

It is easy to see that love is light. Look at the face of a woman who, though perhaps very plain, has fallen in love and knows herself loved in return. That plain face is then illumined and transformed until it is lit up, and literally shines with the light of love. The same is true of the face of a young father or mother when for the first time they hold their firstborn child in their arms. Much more is it the case with the born-again children of light! They are so filled with the light of love that it comes shining out through their faces. The older they grow and develop in love, the more evident it becomes. They are like transparent containers of an inner lamp, the light of which streams forth from them all the time, so that the Lord's description is quite true—they are "a light set on a candlestick which gives light to all that are in the house ... a city set on a hill cannot be hid."

A mind which is continually filled with the light of love cannot help revealing it, for it shines out for all to see. In elderly Christians this is often particularly noticeable, for as the veil of sense grows dimmer and the light emanating from loving thoughts grows stronger, that light often streams forth in the most beautiful and arresting way so that even strangers notice it. Especially is this the case with Christians when they are thinking or speaking about the Lord of love and his Kingdom. It is said of one of the saints of olden times that as he passed along the street a ragged beggar cried to him, "Oh, you with heaven in your face, spare me a penny!"

The opposite, however, is true of those

who love selfishly and possessively and whose minds are habitually filled with the dark thoughts of self-love and dislike of others. Their faces grow more and more shadowed, restless, and discontented. This is not fiction but reality; for we are all mirrors of our own thought habits.

Yes, love is the organ of spiritual sight. It is insight into heavenly realities. And it is no good saying that these things are mere illusions. Illusions do not produce light. They bring shadow and increasing darkness. That, indeed, is how we are meant to distinguish between truth and illusion and falsity. We know the "fruit of the Spirit" by their kind and quality. It is perfectly easy to recognize those in whom the Spirit of truth and love has produced his own fruits of love, joy, peace, longsuffering, gentleness, goodness, faith, meekness, self-control (Galatians 5:22, 23).

A child of God simply cannot afford to ignore the responsibilities of love. The Apostle John earnestly warns us that those who *will not* love develop first dislike, then contempt, then hate of others, and this leads to the most complete blindness. The first and surest sign by which anyone can know that he has diseased eyesight in spiritual things is that he finds himself despising certain people, contemptuous of their ideas, their weaknesses and idiosyncracies, and unwilling to bother about them. All born-again children of God need to keep a vigilant lookout for any such symptoms in themselves, for they indicate an infection which, if not at once treated by the Great Physician, will lead back into a condition of blindness.

As for refusal to forgive one another, this most surely is the most serious evidence of a lack of genuine love. We cannot serve God and at the same time make a habit of refusing to forgive.

The other morning I was walking along the seashore pondering the ever-present problem with which we are all confronted—how to maintain loving attitudes and reactions toward people who jar us, wound our feelings, make continual selfish demands, and whom it seems incredibly difficult to like, much less love! Suddenly I heard a small boy's voice exclaiming impatiently, "Oh, come along, Dad! Let's leave him behind!" I thought how perfectly that attitude of a very nice-looking little boy with an obviously exasperating brother summed up this whole problem of our reactions to others, the temptation to try and "wash our hands" of them, to leave them behind to their own unlovely devices as long as they don't bother us, to look at them through eyes not yet developed in loving understanding, instead of through the eyes of the wise and loving Father of us all.

Only the other day I was shown a passport photograph of somebody I knew. On such occasions it is not generally polite or kind to say, "Oh, what an excellent likeness of you it is!" but rather to murmur commiseratingly, "I would never have recognized that as a picture of you; how simply frightful passport photos make one look!" Why is that? Simply because the photo of us taken in a harsh, glaring light seems to show up every defect in hard lines and to leave no trace of the poorly developed good ones! Everything we would rather people did not notice about us is revealed with unkind prominence.

That is generally the sort of likeness of oneself presented by an ordinary passport photo. But pay the photographer just a little more in order to have the picture "touched up" and then all your friends will exclaim happily, "Oh, what a perfect likeness of you at your very best! I never thought that a passport photograph could be as good as that. Please *do* let me have a copy!"

Now why should that be the case? Simply because the photographer, with an eye to future orders for Christmas cards and possible enlargements, will have done his best, carefully fading out the blemishes and enhancing all the good points which the glaring, harsh light seemed to have missed. In fact, he is helping us to look as he knows we would really like to be, though not even the most skillful art can introduce beauties which are not there and make it still appear as a "true likeness." It can, however, cover a multitude of defects and show us an inspiring picture of ourselves as we would really like to be.

What a message there is here for us! Again and again the Gospels reveal the fact that Jesus looked at people in a special way, not concentrating on their filthy rags or horrible leprous flesh, nor on the self-satisfied smile of some and the marks of sinful living in others.

It seems that he looked at the situation and circumstances in which each person lived, at the obvious handicaps and disorders and difficulties with which they had to battle, such as extreme poverty, illiteracy, disease, physical handicaps, mental disorders, uninteresting work, and frustrations of all kinds which obviously wounded them and tempted them to react and behave in unlovely and wrong ways instead of God-inspired ones. Yes, the things which he instinctively and compassionately looked for were the handicaps and hereditary and temperamental weaknesses or social injustices which made life so difficult for them. It was not the wrong things which people did and the unlovely and selfish ways in which they behaved which drew his attention, but the burdens which everyone carried, which so often seemed insupportable and which wore them out nervously and physically, the afflictions which those difficult people were experiencing which seemed invisible to others or were unnoticed by them. When we look for the burdens which the people we have to live and work with are carrying, their temperamental difficulties, and the ways in which they feel frustrated, rather than at their irritating habits and actions, we too will begin to feel toward them as Jesus did. We shall be "moved with compassion" toward them and long, as he did, to say tenderly and understandingly, "Come unto me all you that labor and are heavy laden and I will try to help you find rest for your souls."

In Revelation 3:18 the risen Lord includes in his message to lukewarm Laodicea these words: "I counsel thee to ... anoint thine eyes with eyesalve, that thou mayest see." Oh yes, how greatly we all need to see, in the circumstances and difficulties and tests of other people, the real reasons why they behave as they do. Not to focus attention on the blemishes and unlovely things, except to see them as the visible symptoms of grievous wounds experienced on the battlefield of life. Wounds which need binding up and healing, instead of being treated with blame or contempt.

I have discovered in my own personal experience that in every case the people I am tempted to find unattractive and difficult have to live in circumstances, or with difficult handicaps and trials, which I myself would find well-nigh intolerable if I had to experience them myself. For example, the perfectionists by temperament who have to live and work under exasperatingly slovenly and imperfect conditions. Those with a passion for beauty who live in ugly and sordid surroundings and perhaps are hurt and humiliated by ugly bodies or disfiguring abnormalities. Those conscious of strong creative ability frustrated and thwarted by circumstances which make it impossible for them to express and fulfill their creative urges. Those with a passionate longing to preach good news, but, like Moses, slow of speech, or handicapped by a stammer or inability to express themselves freely either in speech or writing. Those with strong executive ability who must work under muddled, inefficient, or unwise people who constantly make mistakes. People yearning for love and happiness who have to drudge in the service of cantankerous and ungrateful employers. These are only a few of the frustrating, humiliating, heavy burdens which are largely the reason why people, unable to express themselves creatively, get into the habit of doing it destructively or unkindly or even maliciously, when attacked by the demons of envy and hurt pride.

In the old story of Ulysses and his fellow mariners, all of them princes or the sons of nobles, we are told that after exhausting adventures and hardships of all kinds, they came to an island where lived a cruel enchantress named Circe. She welcomed them, travel-worn, hungry, and thirsty as they were, to a great banquet, and urged them to gorge themselves to surfeit. Then she waved her wand over them and changed their bodies into the likeness of wild beasts or filthy swine and, laughing cruelly, drove them out of her palace to prowl through the forest or to wallow in the mire of the pigsty. When Ulysses came, seeking his lost friends, they rushed toward him in their animal bodies, grunting and howling for help, but quite unrecognizable under the cruel spell which had been cast upon them. He could see only the bodies of apparently savage and disgusting creatures, quite unlike the real selves of his friends and companions. Then Circe, lovely and beguiling, came to meet him too, but he overcame her wiles and was able to break her evil spells. Suddenly, the hideous, bestial bodies of the creatures around him disappeared, and there were his loved comrades again in their true likeness.

Oh, how passionately I, and surely all of us, yearn for the lovely power which only Jesus can give us by anointing our eyes with the eyesalve of love. Then we become able to see with compassion and to cooperate in breaking the evil spells which self-love has been able to cast over poor human beings. Not to see as in a harsh glaring light the sort of unattractive beings which appear generally on passport photographs, but to see everyone "touched up" by the help of loving understanding! For indeed our dear Lord and Savior, "being touched by the feeling of our infirmities," puts forth his hand and touches us and makes us every whit whole. He does this for any who let him. Those who refuse remain beasts.

Let us remember also another glorious and challenging truth—it is through the people whom we find the most difficult to love and understand and appreciate, that we can receive the most help. We are brought into contact with them, perhaps continually, because through learning to overcome our critical reactions and judgments, and to concentrate on their heavy burdens rather than on their behavior, we can grow more and more like the perfect ideal, Jesus Christ himself. They afford us the opportunity to be liberated into the true life of love. By learning to love and appreciate and understand them, we can become overcomers indeed.

Years ago a missionary friend attended a mission conference in the home country and spoke about her work. Afterward a crowd of listeners gathered around her, asking questions and showing tremendous interest in all she could tell them. Then one dowdily dressed woman she had noticed several times, and had dismissed from her thoughts as completely lacking in interest, and who generally seemed rather ill-at-ease, also joined the group and shyly asked a very ordinary and uninspiring question, to which a quick and careless answer was given. The woman then walked away and was quickly forgotten. Weeks later, when my friend went to her mission center to say good-bye just before returning to the mission field, the secretary said to her, "I do hope at the conference you had the opportunity of meeting Miss So-and-So (the name of the lady who had not been worth bothering about), and expressing your gratitude to her. She could not go to the mission field herself and it nearly broke her heart, but she decided that she would pay as much of the salary of another missionary as she could afford by hard work and much self-denial, and you are the missionary she supports."

There were tears in my friend's eyes as she told me this and exclaimed sorrowfully, "Wasn't it awful that I didn't realize, and just ignored her!"

How hardhearted and blind and lacking in understanding we are all tempted to be, and yet shall we not find that when at last we stand face to face with our Lord, the opportunities which we most needed in order to develop in the life of holy love and Christlike compassion, were granted to us through those we were tempted to dislike or despise or resent.

I remember visiting a very special friend of mine, with whom I had lived and worked for the four happiest years of my life in the Holy Land. She is eighty-six now, and for a good many years past has been living in an apartment of her own, with kind neighbors and friends close at hand. As she opened the door to me, a strong smell of burning swept out into the hall.

"Oh, Hannah, darling," she said regretfully and yet quite cheerily, "I have reached the stage when I forget everything. I put the potatoes in the casserole in the oven, and they are all scorched to cinders on one side. But we can cut the bottoms off and eat the tops! How lovely it is to see you!"

She could not hear a word I said until she had found and adjusted her hearing aid, and her dear, kind eyes could not easily see the love with which I was regarding her. But as we ate together the meal which her love had provided, I eagerly asked my questions. We were such old friends that I felt quite free to tell her all that was in my heart, and even to speak of "the unmentionable subject," one's own passing from this world to the next.

"Peace," I said (that is not her name but it well describes her), "do you still read Bunyan's *Pilgrim's Progress*? Especially the part about the pilgrims coming to Beulah Land, on the edge of the River, before they crossed over to the Celestial City. We read that in Beulah Land they anointed themselves for their departure from this world, and there they felt as if they were in heaven even before they reached it."

"Oh, yes," said Peace instantly. "I turn to that again and again, even though I can do very little reading now. The River can't come too soon for me, Hannah, but I am very happy while I wait to cross over."

"What makes you so happy?" I asked.

She did not hesitate for a moment. "As long as you have someone to love, and to be loved by," she said, "you cannot help being happy."

For a moment I was almost taken aback. Peace, like myself, is unmarried. She has no lifelong companion, and no children to comfort her. All the friends of her own generation have passed on into the world of light. She herself was the youngest member of a family of twelve and is the only one left. Then who was there left for her to love and to be loved by?

Well, the answer soon became quite clear. Everyone she met! She had one special niece who had been living near her, but now was preparing to move to the other side of the country and wanted to make a home for her there. "I don't know anybody in those parts," said Peace, "but my friends think I am getting too old and forgetful to live alone any longer, and it will be lovely to live with her. I sometimes feel a little lonely and terribly useless, but if you love you can't stay lonely and unhappy. Remembering others and thinking about them lovingly is something I can still do."

The very first result of the transformed thought-life which I have mentioned throughout this book was a transformation in my understanding of the things I read and meditated upon in the Bible. I began to see all sorts of new and wonderful aspects of the truth to which I had, hitherto, been completely blind. Indeed, I soon began to see new and enlarged meanings and significance in almost every passage of the Bible that I studied. It was as though not only was I myself becoming a new person, but the Bible was also becoming a new book, and was introducing me to a world of glorious truths which I had never suspected existed.

Almost at once I found myself confronted by something which seemed to turn my whole previous world of religious ideas and beliefs upside-down. It began with the Old Testament challenge and command which Jesus also declared was the foundation and summing-up of all the spiritual insights revealed to us through the law and the prophets. In Matthew 22:35-39 we read this:

"Then one of them, which was a lawyer, asked him a question, saying, Master, which is the great commandment in the law? Jesus said unto him, Thou shalt love the Lord thy God with all thy heart, and with all thy soul, and with all thy mind [see Deuteronomy 6:5]. This is the first and great commandment. And the second is like unto it, Thou shalt love thy neighbor as thyself" [see Leviticus 19:18].

I had always disliked and dreaded reading this passage about loving my neighbor as myself, and would have been most thankful if Jesus had said that it was an Old Testament command not binding upon his followers, instead of confirming that it was absolutely fundamental!

You see, I personally had always found it terribly difficult to love human beings. They seemed to me to be so cranky and difficult and annoying and selfish; so *un*lovable in so many ways! This, I had tried to explain to myself, was because human beings are fallen, sinful creatures, not at all what God meant them to be; and, therefore, I ought not to be expected to love them in their present unlovely condition, though of course I should commiserate and feel sorry for them. But as to the command to love them as I loved myself, how dreadfully and absurdly impossible it seemed. How can one love the particularly aggravating and incompatible people one sometimes has to live or work with, as much as one loves oneself, let alone complete strangers, or, worse still, actual enemies, as the Lord's story about the Good Samaritan teaches us that we must do? Alas, there were quite a lot of my neighbors whom I did not even want to like or be friends with. They annoyed and irritated me so much that it had always seemed to me that it was better for them, as well as for myself, if we had as little to do with each other as possible.

But now, right at the very beginning of my transformed thought-life, this command to love my neighbor as myself kept confronting me, and refused to let me escape from its challenge. It made me feel dreadful, because I really did not see how I could possibly obey it.

The principle I had to face is this—it is absolutely impossible for anyone to *do* or *act* righteously unless that person also *thinks* righteously. A righteous man is one who thinks right thoughts and then expresses them, for "as a man thinketh in his heart so he is."

This transformed thought-life develops in us the spiritual sense of smell, or "discernment" between good and evil, as the writer to the Hebrews expresses it. A cleansed mind becomes exquisitely sensitive to evil, smells its approach, and turns from it with loathing as from a stench. Goodness, on the other hand, is welcomed with delight, as a lovely fragrance or perfume. This becomes an unconscious inner reaction, as unconscious as is breathing in the natural realm. No evil, impure, unloving thought can gain an entrance to the love-controlled mind, because as it approaches and tries to enter, the inner man discerns it as though it were an offensive odor. Unholy thoughts, which in our unregenerate days gave us a kind of dreadful pleasure, are now like an unbearable stench. Unloving, critical thoughts are like the approach of something emitting a sickening odor, while thoughts of love and peace and holiness are like "a garden of spices" and sweet-smelling odors, a garden where the Lord of Love "feedeth among his lilies"; the garden to which the apostle referred when he urged us in the "whatsoever" passage of Philippians 4:8 to "think on these things."

For the things that are "true ... honest ... just ... pure ... lovely ... of good report ... [full] of virtue, and ... praise" emit such a lovely fragrance that the "new man" revels in them just as his Lord does, and cultivates them with great delight!

Where are we living? In the selfish world we can see? Or in the Kingdom of God? God is love, and he expects us to be like him.

Read all of Hannah Hurnard's best-selling books.

_____ **God's Transmitters.** Prayer need not be a burdensome duty. It is meant to be a joyful and creative privilege. 75-1085-1-HURD

_____ **Hearing Heart.** An intimate, autobiographical look into the life of Hannah Hurnard. 75-1405-9-HURD

_____ **Hinds' Feet on High Places.** An allegory dramatizing the journey each of us must take before we can learn the secret of living life "in high places." Hardcover 60-1394-X-HURD, or Living Book 07-1429-6-HURD

_____ **Kingdom of Love.** The ABCs of love presented here will enable us to represent God's love to those around us. 75-2080-6-HURD

_____ **Mountains of Spices.** An allegory about human weaknesses and strengths, comparing the spices in Song of Solomon to the fruits of the Spirit. 07-4611-2-HURD

_____ **Walking among the Unseen.** A call to practice the New Testament pattern as the normal standard of life. 75-7805-7-HURD

_____ **Wayfarer in the Land.** An epic of the author's experiences in bringing the Wayfarer's message to remote settlements in Israel. 75-7823-5-HURD

_____ **Winged Life.** This book presents five keys that will transform the way you think and make the "winged life" a reality. 75-8225-9-HURD

_____ **Hurnard 8-volume Gift Set.** 75-1547-0-HURD

If you are unable to find any of these titles at your local bookstore, you may call Tyndale's toll-free number **1-800-323-9400, X-214** for ordering information. Or you may write for pricing to **Tyndale Family Products, P.O. Box 448, Wheaton, IL 60189-0448.**